The Cat Lover

Wendy Owen

The Cat Lover
and other stories

Peter Owen · London

ISBN 0 7206 0104 5

PETER OWEN LIMITED
20 Holland Park Avenue London W11 3QU

First British Commonwealth edition 1976
© Wendy Owen 1976

Printed in Great Britain by
Villiers Publications Ltd London NW5

Contents

To my dear friend Susan Paine

The Cat Lover

Georgina wanted an aquarium. 'It would look lovely just there,' she said, waving her arm in the direction of the corner of the living-room.

The room was already overcrowded: fragile chairs and side tables with spindly legs, about to teeter and fall, miniature altars for porcelain figures, trailing plants. 'You couldn't swing a cat in here,' Henry said, 'let alone a bowl of fish.' He was tall and large boned, shuffling around the small, overheated house, occasionally breaking things. Tears and recriminations would follow.

Although small and plump, Georgina moved with bouncy agility. She often told her friends that she should have been a dancer. She was extremely house-proud, and devoted to her Dresden shepherdesses and their swains, calling each one by name. Henry referred to them as 'Those ornaments'. Today she wanted an aquarium.

'Sweeties, do let me buy one,' she wheedled, touching his arm. Gold charms jangled on her fleshy wrist.

She found the pet shop by accident. A neighbour had told her about a good drycleaning firm in a side street off Knightsbridge. She became lost in a maze of winding alleyways and mews, with cottages and small, open garages. The stench of oil and the sight of the grimy, squatting car mechanics nauseated her. Didn't their wives ever wash their overalls?

Then she saw the pet shop, the lettering on its dingy facade almost obliterated. '*Los Animales*' it said. She read the words aloud.

At first she thought the shop was closed. Then she noticed a shadowy figure moving about at the back. She ventured inside, clutching the clasp of her handbag and peering into the semi-darkness. The heat and the smell of animals overwhelmed her. She felt faint and half stumbled over a box, or was it a cage? Why was the shop so dimly lit?

A bony hand supported her elbow. 'I have to keep it warm and dark in here because of my night creatures.' The man's voice, although harsh, was high pitched. Probably a homosexual. She got on well with homosexuals and tended to mother them. Henry often teased her about her patronage of the hybrid breed: 'You and your arty pansies,' he would say.

The man steered her towards a low wooden chair. She sat down, patted her hair and sighed: 'Actually, I want to buy an aquarium.'

He stared at her for a long time while she, in turn, was able to make out his features. He was very tall and thin, his long face pitted with intense, staring eyes. Brown, lustreless hair sprang from his protruding brow. There were dark stains down the front of his turtle-neck sweater.

'Are you the owner?' she finally faltered.

'This is my shop.'

Every word was an angry emphasis. He turned and

strode away from her down the narrow room. She leaned forward, peering at his silhouette, faintly outlined against the dim light beyond. He was darting and swooping among what must be cages, calling to their occupants. Animal noises, jungle sounds, an endless cacophony welled and subsided.

Georgina crossed, then uncrossed her legs. 'I want a fairly large aquarium with lots of tiny coloured fish. You know what I mean? I had a friend once. . . .' Her voice trailed off. The proprietor seemed to have disappeared completely.

Her mind filtered and distilled anecdotes to tell Henry and her friends. 'You should have seen it, a veritable jungle, absolutely filthy. The owner was completely mad, you've no idea.' Then the man reappeared, carrying a large, dark animal. He dumped it on her lap; it was an enormous black cat.

'I don't want a cat,' she protested, 'I came to buy an aquarium.'

'You don't need an aquarium. This is better for you. He's a tom.' His proud tone and authoritative air impressed her.

The cat jabbed his front paws into her thighs and after a few nervous purrs settled down on her lap and went to sleep.

'Isn't he sweet, he likes me.' She stroked his head and ears. 'He's terribly sweet, but he isn't quite what I want.'

'Take him. If you haven't got used to each other in a month's time, bring him back and I'll exchange him for an aquarium.' His warm, intimate tone surprised her. Perhaps he wasn't a homosexual after all.

She wiped the corners of her lips and each side of her nose and smiled. 'I don't believe you've even got an aquarium,' she teased. Again he retreated. She heard the click of an electric switch.

The aquarium was fairly large and quite beautiful. Shoals of tiny multi-coloured fish darted through the reeds and little mounds of stones and shells. A command performance.

'Aren't they lovely?' She tried not to sound over-enthusiastic, as Henry said this always put up the price.

The man abruptly switched off the light. 'They're not for you. This is your pet.' He almost spat out the words.

Despite her protestations he urged her out of the shop while the cat continued to sleep in her arms.

'He's yours for fifty pence and that's a bargain. If you don't take to him in a month's time, I'll exchange him for the aquarium at the same price, I promise you.' He breathed heavily as he steered her through the side streets towards Knightsbridge, and bundled her into a taxicab.

The fifty pence were extracted with some difficulty as the cat had woken and was now crawling about on her lap. Georgina's gold mesh shopping-net became entwined with the handle of the taxi. At last the door was slammed.

'You'll never exchange him for an aquarium for fifty pence,' she argued and fell back clutching the cat as the cab drove off in the direction of Sloane Street. Her skirt was criss-crossed with hairs. The cat stared into her eyes and purred. He began nuzzling into her groin. 'You funny old pussy, you do like me, don't you!'

Henry was furious. 'You must be out of your mind! My God, look at the size of the damned thing.' The cat had slunk under a chair.

'You've hurt his feelings.' Georgina tried to coax the cat from his hiding place. She was having some misgivings about his strong smell, which she tried to disguise with her 'Miss Dior' perfume.

'I don't know which smells the worst, that animal or the fish you cook for him,' Henry grumbled. The cat's appetite was immense. He ate noisily, scattering flakes of fish over a wide area of the kitchen floor.

In time Henry regained his temper; one had to make allowances for a barren wife. They could not agree on a name for him. 'Pussy' seemed to stick for the time being, although Georgina would have preferred something more exotic.

She bought him a collar studded with red stones. She called him her handsome Pussy. Risking all, she decided to give him a bath.

It was surprising how little he fussed. He mewed only twice, clawing the side of the bathtub. When Henry poked his head round the bathroom door, Georgina was holding the cat on her lap wrapped in a large bath-towel. 'It's like a bloody furnace in here,' he muttered as he stumbled down the stairs.

Pussy's reward for good behaviour was a man-sized portion of English rabbit, steamed in the pressure cooker. She sat rocking to and fro on the kitchen chair, watching him eat, her hands folded over her plump belly. 'Dear

Pussy, we have affinities. I love my food, too.' Henry was a picker, a nibbler, frequently indulging in larder snacks. 'He's our mouse,' she confided.

When Henry accused her of giving Pussy all the top of the milk she denied it. 'We all get an equal share.'

It was late August. The afternoon temperature was high up in the seventies as Georgina lay on her bed taking her siesta. The cat lay sprawled across her stomach and she was unable to sleep as she did not want to disturb him by shifting her position. She sighed and touched his limp paw. Then she caressed his jaw and murmured : 'I wish you were my lover.'

At once her face and eyes were smothered under an immense bulk. She must be having a bad dream. The heat and the weight were terrible. She struggled and tried to scream. Maybe it was a heart attack?

'Please God don't let me die.' A final wrench and she lunged backwards against the quilted headboard. A naked man was crouching at the foot of the bed. Georgina fainted.

When she regained consciousness, the room was whirling about her, pink merging with blue. She tried to focus; the dark blob was still there, slowly revolving. Not a heart attack after all, she had gone mad. She shut her eyes, moaned and tried to pray.

'Dear lady, do not be afraid. It is your lovely words and kind wish that changed me.' The voice was deep and coarse, attempting to soothe.

Some people go happy-mad. Henry would have to put

her into an asylum. Poor dear, how would he cope?
Good housekeepers were a dying breed. He would have
to manage with a daily or a foreign au pair. But they
were worse than useless according to some of her friends,
always breaking crockery and getting into the family
way. She started to sob.

A rough hand caressed her cheek. 'Don't cry, lady.' He
sounded foreign, perhaps Italian. She must be really
mad. She opened her eyes. He was still there, naked and
hairy, looking at her with soulful eyes.

If Georgina had been less well endowed with imagina-
tion, it would have taken her longer to accept his story.

'I am not what you say a common cat.' He sounded
proud, reclining on the side of the bed, gesticulating as he
spoke.

'A wicked landlady dislike me very much. Do not trust
Earl's Court landlady, they are bad. This one, she is a
witch who live in Philbeach Gardens. She is very clever
and make many spells.'

Georgina nodded. She believed in the occult. She
moved closer, gratified that he had covered his private
parts with the eiderdown.

She wiped her eyes and stared. He had what is
described as a 'stocky' figure : muscular, hairy and slightly paunchy. His hair was nice and curly, not too long.

'That landlady do not like me because of her Delilah,'
he continued.

'Who's Delilah?'

The man made a gesture describing Delilah's charms.

'She is the most beautiful Siamese. I cannot help it,
lady, she is very lovely; all the time I want to make love

but it is difficult. That bad woman become angry when I call her Delilah and make this spell, and I change into a man.' He sighed, covering his face with his hands.

Georgina moved closer. 'You poor thing.' Still slightly incredulous, she touched his hairy chest. He grabbed her hand and turned it over, smothering her palm with kisses. Georgina thrilled and needed little coaxing as she snuggled into his arms.

'Do you mean to tell me that you're my own sweet pussy?'

His answer was a muffled incoherence of love bites on her neck. 'Yes, dear lady, I am your own sweet pussy.'

As a lover he was tender and considerate, unleashing a rough passion that delighted Georgina.

'I can't go on calling you Pussy,' she mused. 'How would you like it if I called you Mario?'

He smiled lazily. 'You call me anything you like, dear lady.'

She was about to remonstrate with him for calling her dear lady, when she heard the front door slam.

'My God, it's Henry!'

'Not to fright, dear lady, just say the magic words.'

'Which magic words?'

'I wish you were a cat.'

Gone were the kisses, the human voice. A black cat sat at the foot of her bed, washing his genitals as Henry entered the room.

She decided to call him Angelo. Henry said: 'Why not call him Fatty?' This made her blush with shame. Pussy, alias Angelo, was lying in his new, soft-cushioned basket. His ears flicked and swivelled as he stared at Henry.

She felt relieved when Henry left for his office. The goodbye kiss she gave him was more perfunctory than usual. 'You look tired, my old lovee,' Henry said, 'you shouldn't work so hard.'

'Am I nicer than Delilah?' Georgina wheedled. Angelo scowled.

'She keep running away. Not like you, you do not run away.'

'Oh Angelo, I'd never run away, not from you.'

Angelo disappeared for a day and a night. Georgina's hysterical telephone calls to the police and the RSPCA upset Henry so much that his ulcer started acting up again. When he finally persuaded her to go to bed in the early hours of the morning, she was shivering.

'He's been run over. Those awful drivers,' she sobbed.

'He'll come back.' Henry was exhausted. 'You wouldn't have had all this trouble if you'd bought a bowl of goldfish.'

She set the alarm clock for six a.m., an unnecessary precaution as she was unable to sleep. As she crept from the bedroom Henry groaned : 'She's gone mad, completely mad. She should have had the fish.'

She would never have found Angelo but for his special miaow. It was unlike that of any other cat, a low-pitched moaning sound. Now it was coming from the foliage of a crab-apple tree in a garden at the end of the street.

'Pussy, sweet Angelo, come down.' She snapped her fingers and made kissing noises, but to no avail.

A small crowd had gathered as she heaved herself up

the lower branches of the tree in the small Chelsea garden. Someone called out: 'Come on me old duck, you're nearly there.' He must have been a navvy or some-one equally common.

The slender tree trunk swayed as she grabbed the scruff of Angelo's neck. He clung to the branch miaowing, his fur standing on end and forming a spiky ridge down his back. Somehow she was able to prize him away. As she stumbled to the ground, he scratched her face.

Henry listened open-mouthed when she told him of Angelo's misadventure.

'D'you mean to tell me that you climbed up a tree?' He sounded hoarse.

'I'm very agile. You know Mother said I should have been a ballerina.'

The idea of his plump wife seeing herself pirouetting in a tutu, enhanced Henry's theory that she might be declining into the change, especially as she appeared more flushed and excitable lately.

Later she transformed Angelo, who begged to be for-given for the scratches. However, he seemed evasive when she questioned him about his disappearance, and began stroking her inflamed cheeks. 'My poor lady, such nasty scratches. All I do is go for a little walk. So many streets all looking the same, I do not find my way.'

It was September. They lolled in deck-chairs in the back garden. Henry dozed intermittently, a panama hat cover-ing his face, his bare white torso wet with perspiration from the recent exertion of mowing the small, square

* PRISE

lawn. Georgina cupped her hand over her eyes, smiling as she wiggled her bare toes along Angelo's inert belly. How she loved his large paws and idiotic expression, the tip of his pink tongue protruding from his bulging jaws, his long white whiskers, perfectly curved. There never was such a cat!

Did she imagine it? Or had Angelo been less passionate lately? He fondled her almost absent-mindedly. She must put a conditioning powder in his milk. A visit to the vet, maybe.

The reason for his diminished ardour revealed itself two nights later. Henry and Georgina were woken by an ungodly din in the back garden: howling, hissing and the clatter of dustbin lids. A fight between Angelo and a ginger tom was in full swing. The moon, half hidden by clouds, was just bright enough to reveal the cause of such enmity. On top of the garden wall stood a young female Siamese with a small head and large, pointed ears. A cat born to be worshipped and fought over. It couldn't be Delilah, please God! Henry threw a toothmug of water over the fighting pair and they stopped and backed away, hissing at each other. The female disappeared over the wall, hotly pursued. Henry went back to bed murmuring: 'Bloody cat! We can't even get a good night's sleep anymore.'

Angelo returned at lunchtime the following day. He slunk in and hid under the tallboy in the living-room. Georgina quivered with jealous rage. She would have it out with him later.

He looked sheepish during her feminine tirade.

'You do not understand, dear lady. When I am cat I

am different.' He shrugged his burly shoulders.

'Different! You're sex mad, that's all you are.' She buried her face in her hands and began to sob. 'I'll have you neutered.'

This brought Angelo to his knees. 'Oh lady, not that! Never that! I ask you most kindly.' His frightened face affected her and she forgave him right away. Later she teased him, referring to his 'night on the town'.

She bought him a polythene tray and filled it with cat litter. 'There you are, you fat old sweetikins. This will save you having to go out in the garden.' He protested, scratching at the doors and windows. The weather had deteriorated. 'You don't want to go out in the nasty rain.'

Angelo disappeared. Georgina grieved. There were no hysterics this time, only gentle keening. Henry said: 'Cheer up, old thing.' A week later he came home slamming the front door behind him. He ran upstairs to the bedroom, where Georgina lay with witchhazel pads covering her eyes.

'I'm trying to rest. I've been under a great deal of strain,' she complained.

A warm, furry animal was dumped on her belly. Angelo! She sat up trying to catch her breath. A white, fluffy Persian with the bluest eyes stared at her momentarily, before jumping over to Henry's bed and settling down.

Henry was excited. 'Isn't she lovely? I thought you'd like her. A real beauty and a bargain to boot. You'll never believe it, but the man who sold her to me only charged me fifty pence.'

'Where did you get her?'

'I found her in a dirty little pet shop in a mews off Knightsbridge.'

The cat leaped daintily off the bed and rubbed herself against Henry's trouser leg, mewing softly.

'Funny thing, but she's taken a real shine to me.'

Safer from Fire

After Diana Oliver divorced her husband, she began searching for a lover.

She was thirty-seven years old, and quite attractive in a sharp-featured way, but she felt she would have to move swiftly if she was to find anyone at all.

Her friends and large circle of acquaintances thought she was good fun, though eccentric and excessively talkative. During the past year some had noticed a change in her; her vulnerability and lack of confidence now lay concealed under a veneer of brittleness.

Jane Marsden's husband, Peter, told her that she had become bitchy. He was drunk at the time. Recently, he had taken to leering at her at parties and discussing her potential availability with his men friends.

Her social life continued after the divorce. She was asked to dinner parties to partner the odd bachelor, divorcé or homosexual. The latter tended to use her as a confidante and to pour out their troubles to her, which she found tiresome. The bachelors and divorcés often turned out to be dull and narcissistic, unaware of her problems. She could see the image of her own future in them, and recoiled.

Yet she loved men. At parties she always gravitated towards them after her second gin, striving to amuse and attract. She considered she was justified in claiming their attention as she was surrounded by female company during the day.

Her thirteen-year-old daughter, Jennifer, did little to provide her with consolation and reassurance. She spent much of her time hunched over a pile of comics or records, ate quantities of potato crisps, and was always asking for new clothes which she outgrew with startling rapidity.

Susan, who was eight and a diminutive version of her mother, had lately begun clinging to her with the noisy determination of a toddler, which Diana found alarming.

Lucille, the French au pair, performed the chores in a half-hearted way, concentrating her interest on the various boy friends who flitted in and out of her life.

'All men are ze sime,' she moaned in execrable English.

Nellie, the tabby, was the latest addition to the all-female household. The children had lured her into the house and now smothered and adored her, quarrelling over cuddling rights. Diana suspected that an allergy to Nellie's fur might be contributing to the attacks of asthma which now alternated with bouts of depression, caused by her unpromising situation.

She first met Geoffrey Bellingham at one of her friends' dinner parties. As she had made it a rule not to become involved with any married men, she had so far found the field limited to a handful of ill-assorted candidates. He immediately struck her as different.

He had a soft voice and spoke slowly. As he observed

her over the top of his horn-rimmed spectacles, the expression of his pale blue eyes was slightly enigmatic and at odds with his candid smile. His teeth were even and very white. Diana wondered if they were false.

At first she found his manner a little unnerving. He listened politely and attentively to everything she had to say, yet hardly talked about himself. She talked a great deal that evening and also drank a lot. Someone said that she was a very gay divorcée.

Geoffrey drove her home to her Kensington flat.

She felt sick and headachy during the short car journey, and shivered inside her mink jacket.

He said good night to her on the doorstep and smiled as she groped for her keys. She hoped he hadn't noticed the grubby lining of her evening bag.

The following day Susan was home for half-term and begged to be taken to the cinema. During the morning Diana moved like a zombie as she helped Lucille clean the untidy flat. The French girl's incessant chatter made her hangover worse, and she was glad to be able to sleep in the afternoon during the Walt Disney double feature.

A week later Geoffrey Bellingham telephoned her. The line was bad and his voice sounded flat and distant. He invited her to a Mozart concert at the Festival Hall on the following Wednesday.

Diana was unable to concentrate on the music. Glancing sideways at her escort's profile, she noted his delicately chiselled features and unusual pallor. His spectacles did not conceal the fact that he must be at least five years younger than herself. She tried to imagine what he would be like as a lover.

Later, during dinner, he spoke of his job, telling her that he was senior editor for a firm of publishers. She told him about her broken marriage, complaining about the social pressures and attitudes she now encountered.

'All the married men I know have suddenly turned into sex-maniacs.'

She was flattered by his low-pitched laugh.

'I'm divorced, too,' he told her.

She looked at him with disbelief. 'You look so unscathed.'

She questioned him: how long had he been married; what caused his marriage to break up?

His answers were evasive and she could feel him cooling towards her. She felt hurt and ill at ease during the silence that followed.

'I thought the Mozart was lovely,' she hesitated.

'Which concerto did you like best?' he asked.

She was perplexed, as she had no clear recollection of what had been performed.

'Take a look at the menu,' he said, tossing the programme across the table.

'The violin concerto in A-major, I think,' she muttered. Her cheeks were red as he steered her out of the restaurant, and her head was beginning to ache. She consoled herself with the thought that she was a least sober.

As he drove her home he told her that he had two young sons. This produced in her the familiar twin emotions of maternity and compassion. She found it hard to restrain her tears as she got out of the car.

Before saying good night he said he would telephone her soon.

She sat chain-smoking on the side of her bed, clutching a glass of brandy, wondering whether she was falling in love with him or whether he was just part of her recurring search for Eros.

The alacrity with which her affections welled up and plummeted, disturbed her. She remembered that Paul had once said during a row: 'Your trouble is, you've got the emotional stability of a girl of fourteen.'

During the next few days she became very absent-minded. Lucille took advantage of this and shirked her duties, feigning minor ailments.

'Mummy, do you suppose Lucille is pregnant?' Jennifer leered.

Susan asked: 'What's pregnant?' She held the muddled but exciting view that it had something to do with bottoms and bosoms.

When Geoffrey telephoned, Susan answered.

'Mummy, it's that boy friend of yours,' she piped.

He invited her to a party at the Cheshire Cheese, to be given by his firm to launch a book.

'It's all about the occult. There'll be lots of witches and warlocks, not to mention vampires.'

'It sounds marvellous,' Diana replied.

He was going to call for her at eight o'clock that Friday. It was then Monday.

That evening, when the children had gone to bed, she indulged in a little daydreaming. What would she wear?

The mental inventory of her wardrobe presented itself in order of occasion. Not the black velvet, they'd all be wearing black. She decided on the blue floral chiffon with the turquoise feather boa. It might be a little over-dressed, but the effect should prove alluring. The imagined snatches of dialogue between Geoffrey and herself were very flirtatious although perhaps a little banal. She would be coquettish in her turquoise feather boa. He would be attentive, inclining to flattery.

Her mood affected the children. Susan took advantage of it by waking up during the next two nights and complaining of nightmares as she climbed into Diana's bed with an assortment of teddy bears and dolls.

'You don't listen to anything I say,' Jennifer grumbled. 'You promised to take us to Carnaby Street *last* Saturday.'

They went to Carnaby Street on Wednesday after school, stopping on the way to visit the beauty counter in Swan and Edgar's.

Recently Diana's face had become thinner. Her cheeks had hollowed and lines had appeared on her forehead.

Jane Marsden, who had been a staunch friend during the divorce proceedings and had remained loyal and understanding, was forthright with her advice: 'You must stop frowning or grow a fringe.'

The fringe hadn't suited her. Paul said it made her look like Mamie Eisenhower.

The brassy blonde assistant at Swan and Edgar's looked offhand as she persuaded Diana to purchase a small, golden jar of rejuvenating cream costing six guineas. She spoke of hormones, vitamins and multipotent oils. Diana felt optimistic and confident as they made their way to Carnaby Street.

When Jennifer insisted on buying a button badge with the inscription 'I feel sexy', Diana protested.

'At least it doesn't cost six guineas,' Jennifer sniggered.

Susan settled for a pair of dangling red plastic earrings, and they went home for tea.

On Friday afternoon Paul arrived to take the children down to Kent to stay with his mother for the weekend.

After the divorce they had formed a friendly, bantering alliance which had soured recently when Paul had found himself a mistress. 'She sounds like a younger version of your mother,' Diana had said, cutting short his eulogy.

Today she was elated as she greeted him.

'You look as though you've won the pools,' he remarked.

'She's got a boy friend,' Jennifer said.

Diana accompanied them to the car. As he turned on the ignition, he looked at her. 'Have you jumped on him yet?'

Her 'damned nerve you've got' was drowned by the noise of the engine as they drove off.

Diana's excitement increased as she began to get dressed for the party. Lucille knocked on her bedroom door before entering. She was hoping to be granted an extension of the usual one a.m. curfew.

'You are very kind, Mrs Oliver. I told that to my boy friend. I said "Mrs Oliver is the kindest woman".'

Diana had just applied her lipstick and was studying the effect in her hand-mirror.

'You look so young and pretty,' she added hopefully.

'If you're going to be late,' Diana said, 'try not to wake me when you get back.'

The previous New Year's Eve Lucille had returned from a party at three a.m. and had fallen up the stairs sobbing noisily as she clutched Susan's baby potty to vomit into. Her Spanish boy friend had told her that evening that he was married, with three children.

Diana felt relieved when she heard Lucille leaving the flat a few minutes later.

When she was ready, she posed and smiled at herself in the mirror, waving a graceful arm towards her reflection. The movement caused a slight moulting of turquoise feathers.

'Bugger,' she muttered, picking up a coiled blue strand.

He arrived at eight-fifteen, looking hot and agitated. Diana had been peering through the net curtains in the lounge since eight o'clock.

'I'm sorry I'm late, but the traffic was awful. I had forgotten how many one-way streets there are around here.'

She poured him a gin and tonic, murmuring her sympathies. A tendril of the boa stuck to her lipstick.

As they walked down the alley leading to the Cheshire Cheese, Geoffrey told her that the Public Relations Officer was laid up with a virus and that he was expected to stand in for him.

He introduced Diana to a fat, middle-aged man called Quentin, who was standing just inside the door of the dimly-lit cellar.

Geoffrey's employer elbowed his way through the crowd. 'Where the hell have you been?' Geoffrey started to explain and was lost in a mass of people jostling to get to the bar.

The fat man fetched her a glass of red wine and asked her if she was a witch.

'Or perhaps you are a gangster's moll,' he suggested, ruffling her feathers.

The cellar was filling up and the volume of noise rose. Diana teetered on the toes of her gold evening shoes trying to catch a glimpse of Geoffrey, and succeeded in spilling some wine on the bodice of her blue chiffon.

'Did Geoffrey tell you I'm the sales manager of this godforsaken set-up?' the fat man bawled in her ear.

Diana smiled and nodded. 'How lovely.' She looked with envy at some of the casual clothes worn by the younger women.

Geoffrey reappeared carrying two glasses of gin and tonic.

'Oh, you've got one.' He disappeared.

Geoffrey's employer looked crestfallen when she told him that she was not a journalist but merely a friend of Geoffrey's. He offered her some canapés and introduced her to a slim, dark woman of about forty. She clutched Diana's arm and told her in sepulchral tones about the details of her recent hysterectomy. 'I still get this drawing pain here,' she croaked, touching her groin.

The fat man snatched Diana's boa and draped it round his neck. 'Does it suit me?'

Diana felt anxious and looked around for Geoffrey.

Later he came up, grabbed her arm, and almost pushed her through the door. She had to go back to retrieve the feather boa. The man was reluctant to return it as he had attracted a small crowd of amused onlookers. He clutched her hand in a fierce grip and asked her again if she was a witch.

They dined at a small Greek restaurant in Soho.

'I'm sorry the party was so awful. Simon told me he'd invited a lot of the press. But I don't think anyone expected anything on that scale.'

On the way home he asked her if she was lonely. She felt sorry for herself as she nodded her head. 'Even in this day and age a divorcée is still considered somewhat déclassée.'

'Déclassée! My God, what a quaint expression.'

When they entered the living-room of her flat, she threw her feather boa on an armchair and rummaged through a pile of LP records. Nat King Cole and Frank Sinatra were tempting choices, but too obvious. She put on Puccini's Il Tabarro. The voices of Renata Tebaldi and Mario del Monaco fused erotically with the background hooting of Seine river barges.

She offered him a brandy, but he said he would prefer a whisky.

'I think I'll have a whisky, too,' she concurred. Her hand was shaking as she poured the drinks.

'Go easy, I'll get stoned.' He had been watching her with amusement.

'It'll do you good to let yourself go, especially after that party,' she urged.

Halfway through the LPs and the whisky they

sprawled in each other's arms on the couch.

Geoffrey paused for breath. 'Let's go to bed,' he said.

She ushered him into the bedroom. 'You get undressed in here.' She sounded like a hostess and blushed. She locked herself in the bathroom, dropping her clothes in an untidy pile by the laundry hamper.

The reflection of her body in the mirror dismayed her. It was reddened by the seams from her girdle and brassiere, while the white stretch marks on her hips, the result of child-bearing, looked almost phosphorescent.

Geoffrey knocked on the door. 'Let me in, I want to pee.'

Grabbing a large bath-towel, she wrapped it round her before opening the door. She was astounded when he strolled in naked and fled past him into the bedroom.

She removed a cardboard box from the bottom drawer of her wardrobe. Paul had given her the nightie three years ago for her birthday. It was made of yards of white nylon, with a lace bodice. Intending to save it for their summer holiday in Portugal, she had never worn it. They had both laughed at the label inside. 'Safer from fire', it warned. Paul said it was probably made in Hong Kong.

She almost broke the flimsy shoulder straps putting it on. Then she sat on the side of the bed and struggled to remove her false hairpiece, anchored with so many hairpins.

Geoffrey reappeared. He was holding her girdle between his fingers. 'I don't know how you women wear these things.'

'You should try it sometime,' she muttered.

He lay over her, embracing her with passion.

'My God, your feet are cold,' he murmured, fumbling with the sash of her nightie. 'You ought to wear bed-socks.'

Diana felt so emotional that she verged on tears.

The bodice of the nightie began to irritate her skin. 'Hang on a sec,' she whispered, pushing him away. She sat up and scratched her neck and shoulders. Geoffrey told her to take it off. The irritation spread further down her back.

'I've got the hives,' she whimpered. She got out of bed, writhing in discomfort. Glancing at herself in the ward-robe mirror, she had the feeling that she looked like Miss Favisham.

She fled into the bathroom and wrenched open the medicine cupboard. There used to be some calamine lotion in there somewhere. The shelves were cluttered with small bottles and jars of pills. 'It's a wonder you don't poison yourself with all the drugs you take,' Paul had once said.

There was only a bottle of bath cologne. It would have to do. She dabbed her back and shoulders with a wad of cotton wool soaked in cologne, and sprinkled talcum powder on top.

After a while she returned to the bedroom, carrying the bottle of cologne.

Geoffrey was sitting up in bed, glancing through the Muriel Spark novel she was currently reading.

'Is this any good?' He sounded matter-of-fact.

'Yes, it is,' she muttered as she got back into bed. She sat forward with her knees drawn up and continued to scratch her back.

'You're covered in welts. You should try not to scratch,' he sympathized, dabbing some more cologne onto her back. She began to cough. The spasm worsened, developing into asthmatic wheezings. He slapped her back. This made her choke and tears ran down her cheeks. Stumbling out of bed she groped in her dressing table for her 'medihaler'.

'Get me some water,' she wheezed.

Nellie's tail was protruding from the folds of the bed-spread, which Geoffrey had flung over the dressing-table stool.

'The bloody cat's in here, no wonder. You must have let her in.'

'I'm sure I didn't.'

'You must have, you put the bedspread on top of her. I could kill you.'

Geoffrey looked surprised. He brought her a toothmug of water and sat on the side of the bed, holding it to her lips. She felt like an invalid. She was cold and longed for the warmth of her old dressing-gown.

'I'm terribly sorry, I don't know. . . .' Her voice trailed off. He looked ridiculous, sitting naked on the bed, wearing his spectacles.

Gradually her breathing became easier and she leaned back, rubbing her eyes.

'You look awful,' Geoffrey told her.

Turning on her side, with her face into the pillows, she closed her eyes. She listened to the subdued noises as he dressed. Finally he leaned over her.

'Are you asleep?'

She grunted into her pillow, screwing up her toes, feigning sleep by breathing evenly.

After a while she heard him leave, closing the door quietly behind him. She swallowed two soneryl tablets and slept.

The following day she got up late and lolled in an armchair in a state of inertia.

Lucille looked haggard as she proffered a large cup of milky coffee slopping into the saucer. 'You drink thees, Mrs Oliver, and then you will feel good.'

On Sunday evening Paul arrived with the children. They seemed boisterous, as if sharing a private joke.

He had bought them a new LP pop record. They bickered as they put it on the turntable.

'You look like the Ghost of Christmas Past,' he said.

Diana told him that she had been suffering from asthma. He seemed relieved at her explanation.

'You ought to get rid of that bloody cat,' he told her before he left.

Susan and Jennifer seemed noisier than usual. Throughout the evening they squabbled over the ownership of the new LP. Jennifer had caught a cold and Diana said she needn't go to school in the morning. Susan uttered a howl of rage. Diana slapped her and regretted it when she sobbed and ran into the bathroom.

Monday was always bad. There were beds to be changed and sheets to be washed. Lucille disclaimed any knowledge of the mechanics of the washing machine. She lapsed into French as she stood, barefoot and helpless, with a bundle of wet clothes in her arms.

Sergeant Pepper's Lonely Hearts Club Band was playing at full blast in the living-room. Diana felt tired and nervy. She thought she must be due for her period. 'Turn that bloody thing off,' she yelled as she flung open the living-room door.

Jennifer was lying on her stomach on the floor, munching chipples. Geoffrey was sitting on the couch. A large, fluffy tortoise-shell cat lay on his lap. He stood up and smiled.

'I found this on your doorstep.' He held the cat towards her.

'Mummy, please let's keep him. I don't think ne's got a home. I often see him on my way back from school,' pleaded Jennifer.

'We can't go around pinching other people's cats. Anyway, you know I'm allergic to them.'

Jennifer took the cat from Geoffrey's arms and went into her room, cuddling it and calling it silly names.

They sat in the kitchen drinking coffee. Diana felt wretched. She was wearing no make-up.

Geoffrey said : 'Why don't you call it "Wheezyanna"?' He seemed relaxed and in a good humour.

'Who?'

'The cat.'

'I don't want any more cats.' She sounded churlish.

He stood up and kissed her softly on the forehead. 'Diana. That name suits you.' Then he left.

During the night she was aroused from a drugged sleep. Something heavy landed on the foot of her bed, followed by loud purring and rhythmic clawing on her eiderdown. She half sat up and focused groggily on Wheezyanna's luminous green eyes, before turning on her side and losing consciousness.

The Gentle Man

It began with a taxi shared from Tangier airport to their hotel. He told Frances that his name was Godfrey, and that he had first come to Morocco eight years ago. His gentle, high-pitched voice reminded her of a vicar intoning the Creed. After helping with her luggage, he climbed into the cab and sat next to the driver.

She was startled by his appearance. He must have been in his late sixties or early seventies, but he was wearing turquoise pants and a pastel flowered shirt. His long hair was dyed blond, and was drawn back into a wispy pony tail secured with an elastic band.

He began to tell her about Hamu. One day on the beach a Moroccan youth had accosted him, asking him if they had not met somewhere before. 'Do you know, he used to cycle all the way from his house, which was quite a distance from my hotel, and stand outside my window day after day?' He tried to explain that their relationship was not a homosexual one, that he'd found himself assuming more the role of a parent or guardian. Frances was surprised by his naïveté.

When they arrived at the hotel, Godfrey appeared agitated as he signed the register. He was most concerned to find out whether or not he'd been given an inexpensive room without a bathroom, as he had requested. At one point he even dropped his passport, itinerary and some small change on the floor.

Frances didn't see him again until the following morning. She was lying on a sunbed by the hotel pool, flicking through the *Sunday Times* and trying not to think about David, when Godfrey came up to her.

'Would you mind if I borrowed your paper when you've finished with it?' he asked. 'They're so frightfully expensive here, aren't they? Actually, I'm waiting for Hamu. He did say that he would join me for morning coffee, but I rather fear that he won't turn up. He's rather intimidated by grand hotels and suchlike because of his working-class origins.'

Frances soon realized that, when not on the subject of Hamu, Godfrey was a very cultured being. He talked about music and literature with great insight and feeling, and she found the soft cadences of his voice extremely soothing.

The other guests at the hotel on the whole avoided Godfrey's company, although they were polite towards him and even listened to him sympathetically at first. They were mostly middle-class families, contented enough with their own company. Many left the hotel early in the mornings with picnic lunches, to spend the day in Tetuan or Chauen.

But the American family thought Godfrey was a great source of amusement. The father, a middle-aged New Yorker, described him as crazy old faggot and delighted in doing impressions of him for the benefit of his wife and children, a boy aged fifteen and his plump younger sister.

The two children monopolized the swimming pool

much of the time, shrieking and splashing the guests as they sunbathed nearby. Godfrey found this objectionable and once told them so. But they merely giggled and the boy stuck out his tongue at him when his back was turned.

One evening Frances and Godfrey were sitting in the hotel lounge. It had a depressing air, not unlike a dentist's waiting room. Ill-assorted armchairs were drawn round glass-topped tables, littered with old magazines and a few comics.

As Godfrey spoke, his watery blue eyes darted around the room. His voice trailed off and he stared into space. His hair, no longer drawn back, hung to his shoulders in dyed blond wisps. He flicked it back nervously from time to time, making childish grimaces.

He explained that he had taken Hamu to live with him at his home in Hampstead eight years ago. 'When he first came to London, he didn't do any work although he's a very intelligent young man. He can drive a car and make himself understood in many languages. I think part of the trouble was that I tended to be a bit over-possessive. But now I give him complete freedom.' He looked at Frances anxiously, and for a moment she thought that he was going to cry. Then he told her that Hamu's family wanted him to return to Tangier.

'It's incumbent upon the eldest son to marry a female cousin, you know. That way they keep the money in the family.' Frances imagined that Godfrey had lavished a great deal of money on his friend.

'I was quite prepared to set him up in his own business, running a small garage. He's very mechanically minded. Unfortunately he dislikes responsibility; also, he's not very good at handling money.' He drew out a couple of snapshots. She had expected the young man to be good-looking, but instead he was small and monkey-like, with a worried expression.

Godfrey was the eldest of three brothers. The youngest had died of leukemia forty years ago. 'I was like a father to him, being so much older. When I first met Hamu he was the same age as Michael was when he passed away.'

They had been a musical family. The second brother played the flute in a leading orchestra. 'I play the piano. I even composed a sonata once.' He bit his lower lip and fluttered his eyes, like a child feigning modesty. 'But I didn't keep it up. I don't play nearly as well as I used to, and my fingers are getting rather arthritic.

'We were a very close family. Until I was quite a young man I shared a bed with my youngest brother. My mother was a great beauty; society loved her. She really was a wonderful woman.'

Godfrey kept a strict daily routine. Each morning he arose at six-thirty to take a long walk, sometimes along the road to Tetuan, or on the sandy beach away from the town. On his return he would talk to anybody who happened to be around the hotel pool, describing his walk in detail.

He was afraid to swim because he'd suffered two mild heart attacks. The last one was caused by Hamu's decision to return to Morocco.

'The pool is rather too chilly for me. I don't think it's very clean, either. Those children are quite capable of relieving themselves in the water.' He always sat in the same deck-chair at the end of the pool and read a great deal. Frances envied him his powers of concentration.

She awoke one morning feeling ill and wondered if it was because of the *cous-cous* she had eaten at dinner the previous night. She lay in bed dozing intermittently, taking an occasional sip of mineral water. During the afternoon there was a knock on her door. It was the young English girl who had recently arrived at the hotel alone.

'I heard that you weren't feeling too good. Is there anything I can get you from the chemist? I'm going into the new part of town shortly.' Frances declined the offer with thanks. 'By the way,' the girl added, 'in case you're feeling up to it later, the famous Hamu is on the terrace with our friend. I can't see what he sees in him. He's no taller than I am and looks really creepy. He must be at least thirty, too.'

Later, when she felt better, Frances dressed and went down to the hotel garden. Godfrey was sitting in his usual deck-chair, busily writing postcards. Hamu was nowhere to be seen.

Someone had told her that the hotel was one of the oldest in Tangier. The garden was well-established and exceptionally beautiful, with a variety of palm trees, banana plantains and other exotic plants. She sat on one of the terraces near a datura tree. The perfume from its white, bell-shaped flowers permeated the evening air.

Before dinner Godfrey came up to her. 'I wondered where you'd got to. I do hope you're feeling better. One has to be so frightfully careful in Morocco. Whatever you do, don't drink the tap water. By the way, did you catch a glimpse of Hamu?' He sounded rather excited. 'He was here for quite a long time, you know. He's going to Tetuan tomorrow to see some of his family.' He pulled one of his faces and looked sheepish, adding in hushed tones, 'He borrowed a hundred dirhams from me. I don't know how long he'll be away for, he doesn't always say. Even in London he'd sometimes disappear for days on end without any explanation at all.'

There was a long silence during which Frances felt tempted to comment on Hamu's obvious abuse of the older man's affection. Also, she would have liked to warn him about telling so many of the hotel guests about his relationship with the young Moroccan. He seemed oblivious of the fact that he was becoming an object of ridicule, as well as a bore. But she preferred not to get too involved with his problem.

There were two new guests. A young blonde girl who wore a white djellabah over her bikini, and her American boy friend. They seemed to be deeply in love. Frances and Godfrey watched them cavorting in the pool and Godfrey remarked, 'They look awfully happy, don't they?'

Godfrey reminded her several times that she should confirm her flight back to London. Despite the fact that she told him she'd already phoned the travel agent, he seemed to think it was necessary to call in person. 'There are only three days left until we leave, you know.' She was surprised at his eagerness to return home.

But the English girl explained. 'He doesn't face reality.

He's kidding himself that Hamu is returning to England later, by boat.'

Godfrey gave Frances his version. 'Hamu will never stay in Tangier. He's got too acclimatized to our English ways, and he's become rather spoilt, I'm afraid. He's staying on for a while just to see his family, but he's definitely flying back at the end of the month. He promised me that.'

'But I thought you said he was going to marry his cousin,' Frances remarked. Godfrey appeared distraught and agitated. 'Well, that's what he said originally, but he's a child, really. He can't make up his mind to do anything when it comes to it. No, he'll come back, I'm sure of it.'

Frances went on a day trip to Chauen. She hoped it might revive the happier memories of her affair with David and relieve some of her present misery. They had both loved the small town in the Rif mountains.

The scenery along the route was more beautiful than she had remembered. The road wound through mountains and green valleys lush with pink oleanders. Her fellow passengers were talking and laughing a great deal, like children on a school outing.

Although unaltered, Chauen had become very touristy. The square in front of the large hotel was teeming with coach trippers and vendors hawking souvenirs. She remembered the way out of town to the small tea place by the waterfall.

Near the entrance she noticed three or four oil paintings propped up against the wall. They depicted rather childish surrealist images, although Frances thought the colours – mostly blues and greens – were pleasing. The artist came up to her. He was a tall young man with a beard, incredibly thin, carrying a tiny baby in his arms.

They conversed for a few moments. He told her that he was Swedish, and had lived in Chauen for a year with his American wife. As she was about to leave he pointed to the paintings. 'They're not very expensive,' he said wistfully.

The tea place was cool and deserted. It was impossible to drink the mint tea as it attracted so many wasps. They crawled round the rim of the glass and one even drowned.

Frances leaned back and closed her eyes. David. David. How long would it take her to get over him?

Towards the end of their affair he had begun coming home at three or four in the morning. Sometimes he wouldn't return at all. When she questioned him, he sulked. 'Anyone would think you owned me.'

He started to bring friends home, young intelligent people of his own age. They played the record player and sat on the floor, their heads full of plans for the future.

There was one girl called Anne. She had curiously unmoulded features and large blue eyes. She was quieter than the others. She reminded Frances of the model called 'Esperance' in the painting by Puvis de Chavannes.

Frances gradually became aware of the various boy-girl relationships, although it was not always easy with outsiders joining the group from time to time. They were not in any way parasitic. They frequently arrived with bottles of wine and bought their own food. Sometimes they gave her flowers. When David became attached to Anne she felt desolate. She found it impossible to understand his infatuation. The girl, with her enigmatic smile, seemed almost lifeless.

Late that afternoon she sat by the pool sipping lemon tea. It had a musty taste. 'The water's lousy,' the American woman said. 'A French gentleman told me they fill the mineral water bottles from the taps. If you ask me they get it from the goddamned pool.'

There was less noise than usual as most of the hotel guests were still taking siestas or getting ready for dinner. Godfrey was sitting in his usual deck-chair by the side of the pool. He was staring at the green trellis fence.

The young lovers came running to the edge of the pool. The boy lifted the girl in his arms and threw her into the water, diving in after her. They laughed and splashed each other. 'Do you wanna fight?' he teased.

Godfrey stood up and walked over to the fence. He peered through, then returned to his deck-chair. A few minutes later he was at the fence again.

The noise in the pool reached a shrieking crescendo. One of the bartenders watched the contest, grinning broadly.

Frances looked down at the month-old copy of *Time* she had been flicking through, when Godfrey appeared by her side.

'Hamu was supposed to be here at four o'clock; he

knows that I'm going home tomorrow. I wouldn't be a bit surprised if he's gone off to Tetuan again. He went there the other day, you know, and spent all the money I gave him. He bought new shoes and clothes for his family and came back with only ten dirhams.'

He returned to his deck-chair. She was watching the couple in the pool. They had ceased cavorting and were embracing, slowly revolving around the shallow end.

Soon Godfrey was bobbing up again. How many times did he go to that green fence? Frances began staring in the same direction. Surely Hamu would come to say goodbye? It was one of those rare occasions when she prayed, as she did when her own back was against the wall. The sun had gone down and a cool wind was blowing. The lovers were sitting by the pool wearing white beach wraps, sharing a cigarette. And Godfrey went to and fro. When Frances realized Hamu had no intention of returning she gathered her belongings and went upstairs to her room. She sat on the side of her bed with a damp beach towel round her shoulders for some time, before beginning to pack.

At the airport she met the American family who were on the same flight. The husband was furious because he was unable to exchange his remaining dirhams for sterling. Despite the air conditioning, he was crimson and sweating.

'They don't want you to take this toilet paper out of the country, but they won't change it, for Chrissakes. I know the pound is supposed to be floating.' He narrowed his eyes, looking at Godfrey and Frances. 'I guess it's finally sunk,' he added.

She was secretly relieved that the seats were numbered so she didn't have to sit next to Godfrey. She was weary of his incessant chatter about Hamu. Perhaps telling so many people about him helped to exorcize him.

Godfrey was sitting on the opposite side of the aisle, towards the rear of the cabin. He had tied his hair back for the return journey. He was already talking to a fat, owlish-looking man, showing him snapshots of Hamu. The man looked bewildered and slightly trapped.

Their plane stopped at Malaga to refuel and take on more passengers. The blonde air hostess explained that they all had to disembark for half an hour so that the aircraft could be cleaned and tidied.

In the terminal building two Englishmen were quarrelling noisily. They were both drunk. One of them, in his forties, was dark and good-looking except for his besotted expression. His summer sports shirt was completely unbuttoned. Frances remembered that David used to go about like that in warm weather. 'You look like an emaciated Tarzan,' she would tease him.

Godfrey seemed excited that he was going home. 'I'm looking forward to seeing my little garden again. Last summer my petunias were magnificent.' It was only when they were walking across the tarmac that he mentioned Hamu. 'He'll be coming back at the end of the month, you know.'

The two drunken Englishmen preceded them onto the plane. The hostesses stood on each side of the gangway. One of them said something to the dark-haired man. As

soon as he was settled in his seat he demanded a drink
which the hostess refused politely but firmly. 'We're not
allowed to serve refreshments before take-off, sir.' Soon
voices were raised and two stewards appeared on the
scene, followed by the captain. 'They're nothing but
glorified waitresses,' Frances heard the man shout.
Frances could not hear what followed but later two
Spanish policemen appeared, guns in holsters and carrying coshes, and the man was taken off the plane. Frances
looked back to where Godfrey was sitting. He was clasp-
ing his hands over his ears and his eyes were tightly
closed.

The plane was delayed for a further fifteen minutes
but Frances didn't mind. Last time she had returned
from a holiday, when she and David had been to Italy,
her Burmese cat had disappeared. The prospect of coming back alone to an empty house was making her feel
heavy and depressed.

At Heathrow they waited at the luggage roundabout.
Godfrey's small battered leather suitcase was one of the
first to appear.

On the bus they sat next to each other. Godfrey's
eyes bulged with clownish horror when he recalled the
incident on the plane.

'I've never seen anyone as drunk as that before. But
I suppose I've led rather a sheltered life. I believe we're
getting near Chiswick now.' Frances looked out of the
window. It had begun to drizzle.

Saying goodbye to Godfrey was more difficult than
she had expected. They both said how nice it had been
meeting each other and hoped that they might bump

into each other again. 'London is really such a village,' he remarked. His handshake was limp. 'I expect you want to dash off and find a taxi.'

'Well, yes. Aren't you getting one?'

'Oh no, I seldom take taxis in London. They're far too expensive.' He showed her his disabled-passenger pass which entitled him to travel anywhere on London Transport at reduced rates.

When he walked out of the terminal he looked apprehensively from side to side, giving the impression of someone strange to London. As Frances was driven along the Cromwell Road, she looked back and saw him standing in a doorway near a bus stop, sheltering from the rain.

Sesame

When people asked her why she was called Sesame, she replied: 'My mother was a very artistic person, so she would hardly give me a commonplace name.'

She was pregnant and spent much of her time trying to think of an unusual name for her own child. Her sister-in-law, Edna, sniffed: 'Better if she spent a bit more of her time looking after poor Lennie properly, all that tinned food and those sandwiches, small wonder he always looks so peeky.'

Edna had knitted a bonnet, a matinee jacket and leggings in buttercup-yellow wool. 'There!' She lifted each garment from the layers of tissue paper on her lap.

Sesame stared. 'You are ever so clever,' she said finally.

When Edna had gone home, Sesame danced around the small lounge with the baby's bonnet perched on top of her dry, blonde curls.

Dance a baby diddee,
What's your mama do widdee,
Put on her lap,
Give her some pap,
Dance a baby diddee.

She stopped suddenly and gazed at her reflection in the mirror over the mantelpiece. There were some days when she could see the resemblance to her mother. Childhood, her mother's illness, the hospital a long way from home; and she crying, asking her father to take her there but not being allowed to visit the place. He kept saying: 'She will be home soon.' Months became years. When she died, Sesame, then aged twelve, felt that she was a privileged guest at the funeral. Like many children who do not feel grief, she acted the martyr. Her pleasure in this role was marred by the whispers of relatives discussing her mother's mysterious illness, and what they should tell the child. Her father, a simple, clumsy man, told her that her mother had stomach trouble. She didn't believe him, but never told him so.

She sat in an armchair and began talking to her unborn child. 'What am I going to call you then? A for Alice, Annie; B for Betty; Cathy, Catherine would be nice: D, E; we won't call you Edna, that's for sure, nasty, interfering body, though I must say she is clever at knitting.'

Sesame arrived home from the shops just as Ernie, the butcher's assistant, was ringing the door bell to deliver the weekly joint of beef. Beef that would be roasted in too hot an oven, and carved so thickly that Lennie would have difficulty in chewing it. The second day it would be served cold with beetroot, potatoes and salad cream; the third it would be minced and made into a grey, watery cottage pie.

Ernie grinned down at Sesame's diminutive figure. She was carrying a large, bulky parcel.

'What's that then, Missus, another bun for your oven?'

'You're so cheeky, Ernie Ryan, I am amazed that Mr Selby didn't fire you long ago.' She invariably flirted with the tradesmen; at Christmas she became the *grande dame,* pressing a two-and-sixpenny piece into their hand with a 'buy yourself something'.

As Ernie carried the joint into the kitchen, she began unwrapping the parcel. Several skeins of salmon-pink wool fell onto the floor. 'I'll show her that she is not the only one who can knit in this family.'

Later, Ernie regaled Mr Selby and his son John with the goings-on at Number seventy-five. 'You would think she was expecting quins! It's the colour of those lights and thick enough to make a bleeding rug with.'

Lennie stopped to pick up the strands of wool from the sitting-room carpet, good-natured and flushed from the lads' coarse sexual innuendoes up at the Green Man: 'You really dipped it in this time, didn't you Lennie? That must have been the Friday you was in such a hurry to get home. Here's to John Thomas.'

Sesame struggled out of sleep, she was glad it was a sunny morning, but she had this pain, pain in the groin, she turned over on her back and gasped, her buttocks squelched in a warm moisture, she looked under the bed-clothes and began screaming for Lennie who was down-stairs making the early morning cuppa. The blood around her narrow thighs resembled the petals of a large, red flower.

Everyone was so kind, especially Edna, who moved in for two weeks after it happened. It wasn't easy for her to comfort her sister-in-law, their relationship was strained at the best of times.

Edna, who was childless, confided to her husband, Dave. 'I'm not that surprised, really I'm not, when you come to think of it. After all, she *is* thirty-seven, a bit old to be expecting your first. And the way she kept running around, upstairs and down, I don't want to sound uncharitable, but what with her mother and that, perhaps it's just as well. It's Lennie I feel really sorry for, he's taken it ever so badly.'

Everyone said what a marvellous woman Edna Bignell was, cleaning, and polishing, and mending clothes that hadn't seen the sight of a needle and thread in years. And the meals she prepared! She brought trays of food up to Sesame, and carried them down untouched.

Their few friends and relatives came to visit, bringing flowers and chocolates and speaking in whispers. Lennie sat on the edge of the armchair in the sitting-room. He wept and dropped cigarette ash on the carpet.

'I have never seen her like this before, she won't even let me in the room, the way she keeps crying and yelling, I don't know what I shall do.'

Edna, at the end of her tether, said: 'Why don't you go for a nice walk and leave her to me?'

Lennie obeyed. He walked quickly up the road to the Green Man. Sesame's howls could be heard by all the neighbours. Lennie saw them silhouetted against their windows. Because it was London and he was married to

Sesame he didn't know their names; not that he wanted to, as far as he was concerned they could all get stuffed.

The door of the Green Man swung closed behind him. The noisy, beery familiarity of the public bar was a comfort. On the few occasions he had brought Sesame here, she had refused to go into the place unless he took her into the small private bar at the side. She had peered round the partition at the noisy rabble of drinkers. 'They are such a common lot in there, Lennie, they have even got those awful fruit machines.'

Mike shoved a pint of ale in front of him, he seemed embarrassed. It took a while before he spoke, and then his eyes were downcast. 'Sorry to hear about your Missus, Lennie, that was rough.'

Lennie grunted thanks and withdrew to the nearest empty chair, slopping drink on the marble table. Normally he liked to keep a rough count of how many he had because of Sesame, who would wait up for him. 'I don't like a husband of mine to come home the worse for liquor.'

Mike lifted the bar flap and came over to Lennie's table. He sat down and handed him a double whisky, the first he had ever bought him. The regulars were impressed by their patron's gesture, and some gathered round to stare.

Lennie took a large gulp; it seared his guts and made him hiccup. He insisted Mike should have a drink, more whiskies arrived, his eyes watered in the smoky atmosphere. Mike had returned to his post behind the bar and was arguing with an Irishman who accused him of only being friendly with the bloody Aussies and suchlike.

Somebody sat down beside him and patted him matily on the back. Lennie stared blearily at his new companion, a teenage youth he had often seen in their street, walking a large dalmatian.

'Haven't you got one of those spotted dogs?'

'Oh, Freddie! he's not mine, I'm just his walker. He belongs to Mrs Emerson in the mews.'

Lennie cringed. Freddie's 'walker' was a nancy boy if ever there was one. The spectators looked amused.

Lennie went over to the bar and ordered two drinks.

'One for him,' he gestured with his thumb to Mike, 'you take it over.'

Mike obliged, then he took Lennie by the shoulder. 'Come on, Lennie, it's closing time.' He helped Lennie to the door.

'You remember that song, Mike?'

'No, I don't remember any song.'

'You must remember this song, Mike, we all sang it in the war.'

'Come on, Lennie, it's getting late.'

'That's the trouble, Edna says it's late, too late for Sesame to have a baby; what do you think?'

Mike had disappeared, the door of the Green Man was shut, the last of the drinkers wandered up the road, some to the fish-and-chip shop, some to their bedsitters, some to catch trains.

Lennie was very drunk. The most upright object in sight was the lamp-post opposite. He lurched towards it and clung, trying to shut out the roaring in his ears. Pressing his forehead against the cold metal, he closed his eyes. Yowls and wails, it must be Sesame. Lennie unglued his eyes and shook his head, then reached out to grasp the lamp-post. The pain was excruciating. He was in somebody's front garden, grovelling by a dustbin, God knows how he got there. The lid had fallen off with a horrible clatter. The crying and wailing was not Sesame but a kitten mewing as it struggled to climb out of the dustbin. It flopped to the ground and stood on its spindly legs, facing him.

'Sesame, I've brought you something.' He put the kitten on her eiderdown. It was grey and dusty, and near to starvation.

Sesame smiled. 'Isn't it sweet? Where did you find it?'

'In a dustbin, near the Green Man. Some bastard must have put it in there.'

She picked up the kitten and fondled it, kissing its downy ears. 'Sweet little lamb, did some nasty man put you in the dustbin then?'

Lennie suggested calling it Dusty, but Sesame wouldn't hear of it. The kitten was not to be reminded of her sordid beginnings. She decided to call it Agnes, which was her mother's second name. Lennie was amazed and delighted at Sesame's swift recovery. 'That kitten's certainly done the trick,' he confided to his brother-in-law. Nevertheless, he was unable to call the kitten Agnes, and dubbed her Pussy and sometimes Tiddles.

Sesame purchased a small cat basket and proceeded to knit a blanket with some of the thick pink wool. Although Edna agreed that it would be a pity to waste all that lovely wool, she felt uneasy as she watched her sister-in-law winding it into tight, round balls and chattering away. When she had finished the blanket she gave the rest of the wool to Edna to knit herself a sweater with. 'She will go and get pregnant again and want it all back,' was Dave's comment.

Agnes grew fat and fluffy, and moulted all over the carpets and Sesame's pink eiderdown. Lennie suffered from chronic catarrh, and had frequent attacks of sneezing.

Sesame reproached him : 'If you didn't smoke all those awful cigarettes, you'd be as fit as a fiddle.'

Occasionally he made a clumsy sexual approach but was rebuffed by time-worn feminine excuses. One night he came back from the Green Man and made his usual request. This time Sesame sighed and exchanged glances with her cat, who was reacting to the noisy intrusion by arching her back and highstepping in dainty circles at the foot of her mistress's bed.

Sesame became pregnant again.

'Imagine,' said Edna.

Dave muttered about her not being such a bad old stick after all. The regulars at the Green Man slapped Lennie on the back. 'How about that then, ai, ai, ai, you crafty old bugger.'

Even Mr Selby, the butcher, said he was chuffed. As Sesame left his shop, she giggled : 'I'm feeding three now.' Ernie leaned over the counter and confided to the young Mrs Watson's cleavage: 'More likely four. D'you know, she buys fillet steaks for that ruddy cat of hers?'

Sesame had a son, her own confinement being preceded by Agnes's first litter of three kittens. Lennie's joy was such that he didn't mind keeping the kittens, despite Edna's protestations. 'You should get rid of them before she gets too fond of them.'

'Let's call him after my Dad,' he pleaded. Sesame agreed after a minor tussle, although Bert sounded rather common. But it might be all right if they stuck to Herbert.

Herbert was a delicate child. He would have been difficult to rear even if his mother had been younger and more robust. Edna worried and fretted. Most barren sisters-in-law would have recoiled and declined to give further advice after Sesame's curt 'only a mother knows'. Edna Bignell paused only to change gear, and continued to advise Sesame about dear little Herbert whenever she thought it was necessary. She wrote to her parents, who had retired to a bungalow in Weston-super-Mare:

She has got enough on her plate, coping with little Herbert, I begged her on bended knees to get rid of the kittens. She could give them to a vet or find a nice home for them, but not a bit of it, not her, although far be it from me to criticize. But I have got to hand it to her, she is bringing up our little Herbert like he was a prince. He is kept so clean and has such lovely clothes. . . .

Fourteen months later Sesame conceived again. Jim, the milkman, sniggered to Ernie : 'Imagine having it off with her !'

'Yes, but you don't look at the mantelpiece when you're poking the fire.'

Sesame had another son, much to Edna's disappointment. He was plump and fairer than Herbert, a good baby who seldom cried. As it was her turn, Sesame chose the name Daniel. It was at the christening party that she revealed the reason for her choice. After two glasses of port and lemon she became weepy. 'Dear little Daniel, he was Agnes's hubby, you know. He got run over six months ago.'

2

Herbert, now married, emigrated to Australia and had three children. At first he wrote home regularly : thick, chunky letters with coloured photographs of his family, smiling toothily, posing in front of their spacious bungalow home.

Daniel's whereabouts remained a source of curious gossip to everyone. He moved frequently from one seedy room to another, leaving behind him a wake of unpaid bills and furious landladies. Edna's husband, Dave, maintained that he was no good. There was talk of him having turned queer.

There were now twenty-five cats in residence at Number seventy-five, not to mention a few strays and hangers-on. Cats on window-sills, miaowing to be let in and fed, cats clawing at the front door when Lennie returned from the Green Man where he now spent most of his leisure time. He had retired in every sense of the word. The locals regarded him as a harmless old drunk, who kept himself to himself.

Times had indeed changed. The small cluster of shops opposite had been pulled down to make way for a block of red-brick flats that almost crushed the small supermarket underneath. There was a betting shop that made a bomb out of the regulars from the Green Man. Lennie wandered in there one day and placed two bob each way on a horse called Scrounger. He lost his bet and never returned to the shop.

Some of the cats slept on Sesame's bed, squabbling amongst themselves before finally settling against her hunched-up body.

Lennie moved into the boys' old room. Sesame, now approaching sixty, was secretly relieved as he snored rather loudly and usually smelt of beer.

She had developed a passion for entering competitions of the type found on cereal packets and coffee jar labels. A television commercial for Pussomeat announced a competition. 'All you pussycat lovers have to do is to choose an original name for this lovely feline friend.'

'Ah, isn't she lovely,' Sesame crooned, becoming more and more enthusiastic as a large, white, fluffy cat played daintily with a ball of wool.

Lennie disliked television, preferring the company of his acquaintances at the Green Man. His pub spending, alas, had been gradually curtailed over the years as a result of the large increase in Sesame's family. Now he stared bleakly at the white cat standing on her hind legs to get at the bowl of Pussomeat.

'It looks like one of them abominable snowmen,' he grunted.

'How can you say such a thing?' She was sitting in an armchair, stroking one of her favourite lap cats, Sally, a large, sleek tabby.

Lennie began rummaging amongst a pile of newspapers. 'There is a piece about them in the *Mirror*. The mountain climbers in the Himalayas keep on about them, here it is, large white creatures leaving huge footprints, they call them Yeti.'

Sesame read the article after Lennie had gone to bed and sat quietly puffing on a cigarette, something she rarely did except on special occasions.

A great deal of effort went into filling in the entry form and addressing the envelope. Like a child, she feared she might lose points if her entry lacked neatness. She gave a choice of three names: third place, Pussy-willow; second place, Furrylove; first place, Yeti. The prize was very grand: a two-week holiday in Majorca for two, with all expenses paid, or a large deep-freeze food cabinet. Although perpetually short of money, she yearned only for the glory and publicity that such a prize would engender.

Sesame won. The excitement proved too much for her, and she took to her bed with a bilious attack and shattered nerves. Lennie, bewildered and also shaken, had to cope with feeding the cats and being interviewed by a brittle public relations girl from Pussomeat, who wanted to know what he thought of their new, vitamin-enriched product. She finally concocted a quote for him, assuring him brightly that not only would he receive a year's free supply of cat food, but that his name would be mentioned on the television commercial.

At this point Sesame trotted downstairs in her dressing-gown and heard the final utterance. 'You seem to forget, Miss Whatever-your-name-might-be, that it was me who went in for the competition.' She spoke in her posh voice and glared haughtily at the brassy creature.

The trip to Majorca was out. 'After all, who would look after my lovely pussies?' Edna, with a look of suffering, said she would come in and oblige, especially for dear Lennie's sake, he could do with a nice holiday.

'It is very kind of you, Edna, I am sure, but my pussies are so used to me that they would miss me.' She smiled through gritted teeth before awarding them the sop. 'I thought I would make over the prize to both of you, you would be most welcome to it, I am sure.'

Both Edna and Dave were flabbergasted, to say the least. 'It is very nice of you, Sesame, but I think we'd better go home and sleep on it.'

Waiting twenty minutes for a 31 bus they jogged up and down, puffing the icy air. On the bus journey home their voices rose as they discussed Sesame's proposition. 'I am not accepting charity from her, if that's what she thinks. Apart from that, who wants to go gallivanting round Majorca? It's not that we can even speak the language. They say it gets ever so hot there in the summer, and you can't even drink the water.'

Dear Sesame,
Much as David and I appreciate your kind offer donating us your holliday in Majorca prize, we are unable to accept it for personal reasons.
Yours affectionately,
Edna

She can't even spell properly, sniffed Sesame.

The deep-freeze food cabinet duly arrived. It took up much more space in the kitchen than she had imagined. But despite the advice that she should sell it, she had no intention of relinquishing such a trophy. With a blue felt pen she wrote on the gleaming white surface in large letters: 'In loving memory of Agnes who fell asleep in 1949'.

Sometime later Sesame came down with influenza and ran a high temperature. In between feeding the cats, Lennie took her up cups of tea and aspirin. It was useless persuading her to see a doctor as Sesame had no time for the medical profession. This was largely because whenever she had sought the doctor's advice for her bronchial troubles in the past, she had always been told to get rid of the cats.

She coughed and wheezed a great deal, but was grateful to Lennie for his concern. Towards evening she waved a weak hand. 'You go and have your walk now, I'll be all right.' She always referred to Lennie's trips to the pub as his walk.

He sat at a table by himself, muttering. 'Sesame, deep freezer, cats, bloody dustbin. . . .' None of it made much sense to Jack, the new publican. 'Poor old devil, he's harmless enough, which is more than can be said for some that come in here.'

Lennie got drunker than usual. He had difficulty in getting into his house, dropping his latch-key into one of the milk bottles that had piled up on the front doorstep. 'Sod it,' he murmured, wishing he could control his movements.

He began tiptoeing upstairs to his room, ignoring the baleful stares of a nucleus of cats that had congregated in the sitting-room.

Suddenly Bluebell, a grey Persian tom, streaked down the stairs in pursuit of Mandy, a black-and-white female stray. Lennie staggered, reaching in vain for the balustrade before falling backwards. His howl, lapsing into groans, half woke Sesame, who assumed that Charlie and Paddy were on heat again and were competing for Sally's affections. She smiled and went back to sleep.

The milkman was only mildly curious when he noticed that the front room curtains remained drawn at Number seventy-five. When the neighbours quizzed him about the matter, he was unable to disclose any interesting information.

Edna had seldom visited them in recent years. She had found her brother's company increasingly depressing. 'Poor Lennie, he has gone so funny in the head lately. Not that you can blame him with what he's got to put up with. The smell of those cats!'

Mrs Keen, who managed the small supermarket opposite, was the first person to ask Sesame about Lennie's whereabouts. She had filled her shopping basket with its usual hoard of tinned cat food, plus a few other items.

'How is your hubby these days? I haven't seen him for ages.'

Sesame grabbed her basket, dropping a packet of Kattinibbles on the floor. 'As a matter of fact, he has gone to visit our eldest son in Australia.' She used her posh voice to put the inquisitive Mrs Keen in her place. The effect caused the latter to short-change her by one shilling and threepence.

Two weeks later, Edna came to visit. Tearfully Sesame told her that Lennie had run away. Edna was astounded. The two women began to quarrel, dredging up past scenes that had chequered their relationship.

Later Edna sobbed to a disbelieving Dave. 'Our Lennie running away like that. Poor thing, he must have come to the end of his tether.'

It was Dave who said that the police had to be notified.

Meanwhile Sesame had told the neighbours that Lennie had gone to visit an aunt who lived in Scotland. Two languid constables duly appeared at Number seventy-five and were spotted by Mrs Keen, who nearly fell off her stool with excitement. She short-changed a customer, this time by accident, explaining, 'It's her over the road, her husband's gone missing, isn't it a shame.'

Edna wanted to send Herbert a telegram. She drafted one and showed it to Dave.

'Dearest Herbert, Your Dad has disappeared, if only we knew where, please come home quickly, Your loving Edna.'

Dave abbreviated it to 'Dad disappeared, come home, Edna', which reduced Edna to noisy tears.

'You're that mean. If Herby got a telegram like that, why, the shock would kill him.'

They finally compromised with a hastily scrawled air-letter from Edna, containing many vindictive criticisms of Sesame alternating with sentences as 'not that I like to say a thing against your mother, I know she is your own flesh and blood, but she must have been feeding fifty cats at least.'

Dave's PS was squeezed alongside his wife's ravings : 'You'd better come home old son, something fishy's going on.'

Sesame opened the door and stared at her son. 'Fancy seeing you after all these years.' Her voice sounded bleak and she was obviously shaken.

She kept him on the doorstep, jabbering nonsensically for some moments. 'I hope you don't find your old mother has aged; I've done my best, after all.'

She patted her dry, frizzed, yellow hair. 'I daresay you don't find our English climate much to your liking after sunny Australia.'

Two cats sidled past her legs and ran down the steps. 'They're just two of my pussies. I hope you like pussies, Herbert dear, I have got quite a few, you know. Dear little things, so much nicer than most people I know or care to mention.'

Grabbing his suitcases, Herbert pushed past her, muttering 'Jeez, anyone would think I was just one of the flaming tradesmen.'

Sesame and Herbert finally sat down to their discussion about the possible whereabouts of Lennie.

'He has gone,' she sobbed, 'don't ask me where, I would tell you if I knew.'

Edna and Dave came round the same evening. Edna's arthritis was particularly painful that night, so her husband had been prevailed upon to hire a taxi. A minor haggle with the driver over the small tip set them up for the ensuing family row. This finally reached such a pitch that Herbert raged out of the house, slamming the front door behind him.

'The cheek of the bastards, having a go at me like that, telling me I'd been a rotten son not writing home often enough. Didn't I always send them food parcels at Christmas, and cards too? What was the point? They weren't interested in my new life, anyway. When I wrote to tell them about my sailing boat and how we all took Christmas dinner down on the beach, Mum writes back telling me that roast turkey eaten on the beach in that heat would probably be off, and she wouldn't like to give it to her pussies. As for Dad, he never wrote at all except to scrawl at the bottom of a Christmas card.'

Chief Inspector Turner from the CID called. Sesame thought he was ever so nice, nothing like what you'd expect. She even made him a cup of tea. Her replies to his enquiries were contradictory and muddled. Occasionally she burst into tears and became incoherent.

After the Inspector had gone, Herbert led his mother upstairs to her room. He peered through the net curtains of the bedroom window to the street below. 'You wouldn't think that a place like this could change so much,' he muttered.

Sesame blew her nose and stared at the back of her son's head. She remembered his silhouette as a child. The short, stubbly, fair hair, the protruding ears, like a cardboard cut-out. She recalled it with little affection, and the vaguest sense of guilt. Herbert hadn't been a loving child. Not like Daniel, who had been quite different. You could cuddle him and he didn't mind a bit; he even helped to look after the pussies. In many ways he was like one of them, good and quiet, soft spoken, even secretive.

'Why don't you go and have a nice time now that you've come all this way? You could look up some of your old friends?'

There were no old friends, but Herbert, encouraged by his mother's advice, was eager to get acquainted with the new. To get out of the dingy, cat-infested house with its appalling smell and see old London with its bright promise and mini-skirted Sheilas, was fair galah. Why not enjoy himself? He would never get a chance like this again.

Herbert didn't particularly like the Green Man, although Jack was a decent enough sport who kept asking after his Dad. He soon discovered the pubs in Chelsea and the Fulham Road, where everyone loved the bloke from down under who bought round upon round of drinks.

They stood giggling on Sesame's doorstep, boys and girls, most of them younger than Herbert, with the exception of one intense little woman in her thirties. Her name was Peggy; she had told Herbert that she taught clay modelling and was interested in eastern philosophy. He'd plied her with gins and tonics, wishing that she had been a bit easier on the eye.

Once inside the house, a chap called Bill turned on the radio and they started lurching around the lounge.

'Whatever you do, don't wake my Mum or there will be hell to pay,' Herbert muttered thickly, turning down the volume.

'Jesus, look at those cats. I thought this was an Australian hang-out, where are the flipping kangaroos?'

Herbert grabbed Peggy's hand and squeezed it. 'Come on, Peg me old darling, give us a hand with the beer.' Dumping the large cans on the floor, he shut the kitchen door behind them and switched off the light.

Peggy clung and kissed with the voracity of the lonely and repressed, while Herbert's hand worked its way roughly under her skirt and up her side, squeezing her breasts.

Someone opened the door. 'Where's the bloody beer?'

Peggy dashed the hand from her groin and yanked down her skirt.

'What's all this then? Sorry to butt in on something interesting.'

Peggy glared at the young, male interloper. 'I think we ought to chill the beer for a while, don't you?' Her voice was high-pitched and authoritative. She indicated the deep-freezer cabinet with a wave of her hand and a glance of anticipation towards Herbert.

'There's no room in there. It's full of bloody frozen cat food and stuff, besides which Mum's got it pad-locked. She won it in some barmy competition and won't let anyone touch it. Sorry, my old matey, we'll have to drink it warm. English style,' he added sarcastically.

He opened a couple of cans and retired to the lounge. 'Can you imagine anyone having a whopping great freezer like that, living the way they do? Just the two of them in a bloody cold country like this? My Betsy and I haven't one as big as that with a family of our size!'

Peggy winced at the mention of Herbert's family in Australia.

'I thought you said earlier that your father had disappeared into the blue?'

Herbert wasn't listening. 'I didn't come all the way on a wild-goose chase to drink bloody warm beer.' He stood up, lurching, and went into the kitchen.

Later he returned with a wooden tool box. 'Right, me old darlings, who wants their beer on ice?'

'We do, good old Herby.'

Although the padlock was small, several of the men had a go, hammering and chipping away, damaging the pristine white enamelled surface of the freezer. They were encouraged by the girls, and when it was finally opened with yelps of delight, the remaining pippins of beer were thrust into the frozen interior.

Around two-thirty a.m. Herbert tired of Peggy's probing analysis of what she imagined to be his deep-rooted psychological problems. There was that young Susan, whose boy friend had passed out on the sofa. She wasn't bad at all, a bit shy and needed encouraging, but what a pair she had!

Herbert shuffled away from Peggy and asked the girl to dance. Somebody had turned out all the lights except for a small table lamp. Peggy, wall-flowered, watched the couple slowly gyrating around the room to the music. When it stopped they were still swaying to and fro on the spot, snuggled up against each other.

She went over and grabbed the girl's shoulder. 'Sue, be an angel and help me with the beer, it must be quite cold by now.'

They lifted several cans out of the freezer and Peggy located the can opener underneath a tea towel. Together they opened the frothing cans, filling the outstretched glasses and teacups, many without handles.

Everyone in the kitchen was talking and laughing. Peggy stared at Herbert, who met her gaze.

'Good old Peg, you are like my Betsy, you would like my Betsy.' Then he grabbed Susan by the arm and steered her back into the semi-dark sitting-room. Peggy heard her laugh at some remark of his.

She leaned against the kitchen wall and stared out of the window beyond. There were no trains back to Ladbroke Grove at this time of night. None of the characters in there would give her a lift home, even if they had cars. Not that they would be in a fit state to drive! And it was not the kind of set-up where you could doss down on the floor for the night.

The cumulative effect of the gins and beers had made her very thirsty and her head was aching. A glass of iced water, and then she would start walking home, perhaps grabbing a taxi when she got too tired.

The small fridge was a dead loss for a start. A couple of open tins of cat food, milk and solid butter, but no ice cubes. There was lots of ice in the freezer, though; all you had to do was to scrape it off with a knife.

She was mildly curious about the large plastic bag. With a kitchen knife she scraped off some ice and prodded the surface in one or two places. Ice chippings tumbled onto the kitchen floor, mingling with beer cans. She stared disbelievingly at first, then screamed hysterically. Herbert tried to shut her up in vain. Then he saw the arm and the gnarled fingers protruding from the bag. He fell forward.

Sesame sat in an armchair, nursing one of her favourite strays, a black cat called Prudence. She was trying her best to explain to Herbert and Chief Inspector Turner what had happened.

'I came downstairs one morning and found your poor

father lying there, he must have tripped over something.
I am not one to speak ill of the dead, but you know
he used to take a drop too much quite often.'

Herbert's 'Jeeze, could you blame him?' was ignored.

'He was a dead weight, I couldn't move him an inch,
I'm not very strong, you know. Dr Benson's been telling
me for years that I'm anaemic, but I didn't want to worry
anyone.' She looked at both men, hoping for a bit of
sympathy.

Herbert was pale, his mouth drooped as he stared at
his mother. The Chief Inspector, who seemed so friendly
the last time he came, now looked at her with cold, narrow eyes. She couldn't even offer him a cup of tea this
time.

'Anyway, I was just about to phone your Auntie Edna
and tell her the sad news when Lulu went over and started to lick the blood from your Dad's head, where he had
banged himself when he fell.'

Herbert groaned, covering his face with his hands.
Prudence had vacated Sesame's lap and was clawing
playfully at his trouser leg.

'Herbert, luv, where is that little rubber ball? She
wants a game.'

'I should like to go on with this enquiry, if you don't
mind,' interrupted the Inspector.

'Well, Lulu always did like her meat on the raw side.'

Herbert left the room hurriedly; he felt rather sick.

'That's when I got the idea. After all, a funeral costs
quite a bit of money these days. I was talking to Mrs
Griffiths a while back, and she was telling me about
when her own mother had gone over to the other side.'

'Could you please tell me about your husband, and try not to stray?' The Inspector's voice sounded strangulated.

Sesame looked as if she were about to cry. 'Stray! Fancy you saying that. Lulu was a stray, near to starvation she was.'

'About your husband, Mrs Stokes.'

'How would you like a nice kitten, Mr Turner? Susie is expecting again.'

The Inspector croaked: 'Could you please stick to the point? I must have some more details concerning the death of your husband.'

'He fell, you know, headlong down the stairs.'

Herbert had returned and was pacing up and down the small room, running his hands through his hair.

'Mum, the Inspector wants to know who put him in the freezer.'

'Oh that! Why didn't you say so? I didn't tell you, Mr Turner, how I won that freezer in the competition. Although I wouldn't say it, I must admit it was one of the proudest moments in my life.'

'Why did you put him in the freezer, Mrs Stokes?'

'Well, what with the price of cat food and one thing and another, it's very hard for someone in reduced circumstances to make ends meet, you know.'

'Oh Jesus, you weren't going to feed him to the bloody cats?'

A large pregnant tabby ambled into the room and nuzzled against the Inspector's legs.

'Poor luvvy, she wants her dinner.'

'Mrs Stokes!'

She stood up with arms akimbo and stuck out her jaw.

'You wouldn't shout at me like that if my Lennie was here. Just you try making ends meet with the family I've got to feed! I wonder how you would manage.' She stalked out of the room, slamming the door behind her.

Herbert said in a tired voice: 'Could you come back another time? I don't think I can take any more for the time being.'

'I am sorry, Mr Stokes, but we have to get to the bottom of this. There may be serious charges brought against your mother.'

'Look mate, she may be barmy, but she never done the old man in, that's a dead cert. My Aunt Edna wrote and told me that Dad was drinking like a fish for years, and you don't have to be plastered to fall over cats in this house.'

During the inquest that followed, Sesame went over the whole story again. The audience in the small coroner's court appeared to be held in her thrall. Finally, a report was made to the effect that Mrs Stokes's behaviour was due to diminished responsibility. Herbert was advised to have her committed to an asylum, but he didn't agree. After all, the old woman seemed harmless enough, it wasn't like she had murdered the old man or anything. Sesame agreed with alacrity to attend the psychiatrist's outpatients' clinic for therapy. He seemed such a nice young man, better than that Mr Turner, who kept interrupting all the time. She felt she wanted to do something nice for Dr St John, give him a special present or something, he seemed so refined.

Dear Herbert,

I hope you had a nice trip home. It was such a nice surprise seeing you again after all these years, if only Daniel would come home and see his mother sometimes. I go and see that nice Dr St John twice a week. He is ever so understanding. I have got a nice present for him.

Yours affectionately,
Mother

The nice present was one of Susie's litter. Dr St John wanted to have it put down or give it away, but his wife wouldn't agree to it under any circumstances.

John's Story

To J. who told me

He would always remember the day. His father, a violent man, had never been so mad. He'd kill them both, he said, and he meant it. Father O'Rourke's anger would not be forgotten either. But this was different. John stood there, white-faced, chewing his lips. He thought he was going to die, or faint at least.

Michael, his brother, had said that they'd be all right if Father O'Rourke didn't send off that letter. And so they prayed.

Michael Callaghan was thirteen, John was twelve.

It had started in the school playground. There was a great deal of oath-taking amongst the boys. All the girls stood over by the bicycle shed, giggling.

Whatever it was, it was going to be great.

He and his brother had never been popular, nor unpopular come to that. Just left out of things. Sometimes they were teased about their lumpish hand-made sweaters and outsize trousers, or because they were always together. 'Stuck together like shit on a baby's shawl,' Patrick Bainton once said. He was a big boy, and one of the ringleaders of the gang.

Michael, the braver of the two, had gone up to Patrick and asked to be let in on the secret. He tried bribing him with sweeties and cigarettes.

'Sure an' you'll tell your daft brother, and he's bound to blab.'

It was agreed that the Callaghan boys were not to be trusted. But they could help a bit if they wanted to.

'We're in luck, laddie,' Michael whispered, squeezing his brother's hand.

It was not to be on that day, but on the next. There wouldn't be so many Fathers around – spying priests, Michael called them – because of a special mass sung to give thanks for the money they had collected for the new dormitory.

The boys and girls drew lots from a pair of boys' blue caps. There was a great deal of shrieking and giggling as each unfolded his tiny square of paper. John wondered what it was all about.

Little Maureen Ryan groaned : 'Jasus, Martin Duffy !' Michael said they must be choosing members for a gang.

And Molly O'Shea was in on it, too. Plump Molly, with her thick black hair and blue eyes. John knew her every mood and would lean forward lest he miss a word of hers.

At home Michael would pester him, proud of his brother's sentiment : 'You've got a notion of her.' Not that it helped him get over his shyness in front of her. He would mumble if she spoke to him, and she would turn to her friends, covering her mouth with her hand, telling them.

The day was bitter, windy too. There were great dark clouds. 'Don't let it rain today.'

Nearly all the class were in a stir, like it was the end of term. John kept turning round, looking at Michael. And he would grin and wink.

They all kept dropping their slates, like part of a code, and the girls were giggling. Their teacher, a young priest, never much of a one for discipline, pleaded and threatened. 'The green one,' Patrick Bainton called him.

The bell went. Slamming of desk lids, and running to be first in line for dinner.

John was near the end of the queue, Michael behind him. He pinched his arm. 'This is us, ladeen,' he whispered.

'What do we do?'

'Wait, and I'll tell you.' The line of boys and girls was moving now, fidgeting and suddenly quiet.

Dinner with its mushy cabbage and bacon was soon eaten. Grace was sung before and after. Benches scraped back against the wall.

Into the playground. No Brothers today. Only prefects huddled in corners, telling each other dirty jokes and smoking cigarettes concealed in the palms of their hands.

Michael took him into the bicycle shed and told him what to do. Pointing behind the green and brown tiled lavatories he whispered: 'We're to keep in dick, in case someone comes. If they do, whistle.' He put his fingers to his mouth and frowned. 'Got it?'

John nodded. He was to guard the boys' lavee, and Michael the girls'. The girls' entrance was more risky because it was near the school. John would be able to look through the railings in case anyone came that way.

Although glad of the safer look-out, he still wanted to know; but there was no time. A group of boys, led by Patrick Bainton, came towards them. After a moment Martin Duffy left the others and went up to Michael. He was tall and thin, with red, wavy hair. Ginger Nob, Michael called him. Most times his face was pale and his eyes looked sleepy. Now his cheeks were pink and even his walk was different. Like he was the leader. More like Patrick.

'You lads ready?'

Michael nodded. John looked at him, then at the others. Some of them were grinning, the rest looked serious and a bit scared. John felt scared, too. Supposing they got caught?

Patrick gave them each a Woodbine. They were crumpled from his trouser pocket.

John blushed as he tried inhaling the smoke. He thought they might laugh at him. But they stood there.

'You know what to do?'

'If anyone comes. . . .'

'Jasus!'

'We'll all get slaughtered if. . . .'

'Just whistle, bloody whistle if you even think.'

He didn't care anymore that he wasn't to know the secret. He kept nodding and grinning and nudging Michael.

Now he stood guarding the entrance to the boys' lavatory. The cigarette had gone out. Not to mind, it made him feel sick anyway.

Mostly they were quiet behind there. Sometimes he

heard a girl's voice, but not much else. He began to feel cold and let down. He kept looking to where his brother stood. His head was turned towards the closed school door. He wanted to call out, softly mind you, just so as Michael would turn round and grin. He tried scraping the heel of his shoe on the concrete. The wind was terrible. He hugged his shoulders and his feet were icy cold. He did not dare stamp them up and down. He tried to think of Molly O'Shea. The talks and walks he had with her when he dreamed away in arithmetic lessons. Nights at home, lying on his back in the bed with Michael, who never lay still at all and snored like a pig when he did. His dreams were stale and frozen.

The bell.

He was last in line. Shuffling, stumbling back to the desk he shared with Vincent Duffy. It was no good looking to him for a clue. He wasn't in on the plot at all. His brother Martin's ghost! Silly tinker, coming to school without any shoes. Pinch him, tease him, sure to God he'd start to cry and blab, sod him! There he sat now, leaning over his slate, scraping for all he was worth, with his bottom lip hanging and his nose as red as a beetroot. Who could read that scrawl?

Two days later they were found out. One of the girls had blabbed to her mam. Patrick Bainton said: 'Holy Mother of God!'

There was the devil to be paid.

The Abbot came into the classroom with all the other Fathers, and they all carried birch rods. The door was shut and bolted. They were dragged from their desks and made to bend over, every one of them.

Then questions. Jasus, how many questions! Worse than the whippings. Patrick Bainton got the worst of it; Father O'Rourke kept hitting him across the face with his hand. When the big lad started to cry, John wet himself.

Then they made them kneel down and pray to the Blessed Virgin for forgiveness, before they could even pull up their trousers or knickers.

Father O'Rourke sounded hoarse when he told them that all who'd done such a wicked thing would get letters sent to their homes.

Patrick Bainton, well, he was to be expelled. The girls all crowded together in the corner of the classroom, blaming the boys. And they couldn't even look at the girls.

On the way home John left his brother behind and caught up with the other lads, trying to hear what they were on about.

One word they kept saying.

Late that night, in the dark : 'What's fackin?'

'Hush now, go to sleep.'

They couldn't sleep.

'You filthy divils!' Their father grabbed the old sword from off the wall and smashed it into the fireplace until the sparks flew. Their mother fled upstairs and shut herself into the bedroom with the girls. She'd never done that before. Always she'd side with him when there was a row. John felt faint.

'If one of those letters comes to this house, I'll slaughter the both of you.'

Two days, three days, a week went by. Praise be to God, the letter never came. Letters, circulars mostly, slid through the letter box. Dry-mouthed he watched his father open them.

Months later Michael was to tell him about it. Now that he knew about fackin and babies and that. Now that he could tell a dirty joke himself, and smoke like the other lads.

He could scarce believe him, made him tell it over and over. And his excitement grew.

Little Maureen Ryan, why, she had been paired off with that great slab of a Martin Duffy. And she so small that she had to stand on a bucket, Jasus!

'Who did Molly O'Shea get?' He tried to sound like he didn't mind. Michael said he thought it was Peter Brennan, but he couldn't swear to it.

He looked at her sitting at her desk. She smiled at him, smoothing her hair, and he went on looking and not forgiving.

He heard later that the Bainton family had moved to Mullingar, that Patrick Bainton was working as a garage hand. Which was a pity, as he was a clever lad and had talked of becoming an engineer.

John grew tall, taller than Michael. A strange one, not a great mixer, no longer afraid of his father.

When he left school, he got a job in Powell's store,

in the bedding department.

Michael was always in and out of work. A talker, he missed his brother's company, spending much of his time in pubs, buying rounds of drinks for new friends. He would beg them to stay. With pint mugs slopping and young girls hanging on their arms, they would listen when he told them about the time.

Molly O'Shea married one of the Finnegan boys. They all got drunk at the wedding. Someone said: 'Do you remember when we all went behind the lavees?' And she went red as a beetroot and said: 'I don't know what you're on about.'

John was promoted to manager of the bedding department at Powell's. And Maureen Ryan became a nun.

Bedtime Story

June Trent could hardly believe her good fortune. The first long dress matched her fantasy – pale pink taffeta and net, ribbons slotted through the bodice, little bows and puff sleeves. Furthermore, it fitted her perfectly. Her mother had mentioned the dress quite casually a week before the Christmas dance. 'Mrs Muswell has got one that Sheila has grown out of; she says you can have it if you like.' June received the news with little enthusiasm, after years of having to wear her older sister's cast-off clothes because of the war and rationing, and having to feel patriotic about it. She put the dress on numerous times, posing before her father's cheval-glass, mouthing witty and romantic things to say to Jack Beeston, who was sure to be at the dance.

She had fallen in love with him about four months previously, one of those secret passions imbued with guilt and frustration. He was swimming from a creek nearby one hot September afternoon, accompanied by three or four other youths who started showing off for the benefit of the Trent girls and their crowd. June couldn't stop gazing at his lean body and graceful diving display. 'I might have guessed that mob would be here,' her older sister Diana complained, after being deliberately splashed and getting her hair wet. She refused to wear an ugly bathing cap in the presence of her boy

friend, Eric, preferring to pile her long blonde hair on
top and keeping her head well above water level. Although amused at his friends' antics, Jack Beeston had
declined to join in; he was treading water some distance
away and June fancied that he smiled at her. Since that
day she had begun to daydream about him almost non-
stop. They would go cycling together into the New
Forest, eat a picnic that she had prepared – lavish and
tasty eats, almost black-market delicacies. Never having
heard his voice, these were wordless idylls. He would
reciprocate by taking her to the pictures at Southampton.
At night she lay on her right side, hugging herself with
his strong arms.

'If you keep putting that dress on before Saturday, it
will look even more second-hand,' was Diana's comment.
Eric giggled. 'Enter Miss June Trent in last year's
shredded remains.' Diana was making her own dress of
pale blue art silk. She scowled with concentration as she
stitched a curly motif of blue sequins round the sweetheart neckline.

On the night of the dance the sisters came downstairs
and stood before their parents. 'That frock of Sheila's
looks very nice indeed,' Mrs Trent remarked as she sipped
a sweet sherry. Raspberry nosed, uncomfortable in his
dinner jacket, Mr Trent complimented both girls on
their appearance. He smelt of mothballs and bay rum.
Then Eric arrived, lank black ridges of Brylcreemed hair,
blotched with acne, but cheery as ever. He deposited

a self-conscious kiss on Diana's cheek and told June that she looked fetching. Pump-handling the Trents' outstretched hands, he sat down on the edge of an armchair while Mr Trent was imbibing the second whisky of the evening. He was setting himself up for duty dances with company wives whose husbands he over-lorded. Mrs Trent gave Eric a small sherry and one of her smiles. 'We don't want to get tiddly before we get there.' She had lipstick on her teeth.

The village hall was crowded, festooned with worn-looking bunting. The sudden silence when the Trent party entered was followed by sycophantic nudges and whispers. Then the bandleader, having spotted Diana, struck up 'In my sweet little Alice-blue gown', and Diana, flushed and simpering, sat down on a chair by the wall patting her hairdo.

Much of the evening June was something of a wall-flower. Normally she would have cared, but tonight the dress more than compensated for her lack of dancing partners. In any case she considered most of the village boys to be awful, huddled round the bar in their blue serge suits, with their red country faces. She joined in the Paul Jones, the Ladies' Invitation Waltz, and the Snowball Dance. She was sitting next to Eric, who was giving Diana a long-winded account of his intended career in the Royal Air Force, when Jack Beeston slouched past, looking decidedly blasé with a cigarette dangling from the side of his sullen lips. June felt her cheeks redden and stared down at the floor, wondering if he suspected anything. Diana was still looking at Eric with wide-eyed concentration, having read in a magazine that men adored women who were good listeners.

During the refreshment interval the members of the village band mopped their foreheads and clomped down the steps of the platform to join the throng at the other end of the hall. Their hurdy-gurdy grindings and mechanical beat were a joke among the younger set, who referred to their playing as chamber-pot music. Mrs Trent wafted over to the leader, her slim figure in its pre-war coral georgette gown watched with envy by the village wives. She told him that the music was as splendid as ever.

June found herself encircled by her parents and their friends. Munching a fish-paste and cress sandwich, she was swallowing some orangeade when her mother introduced her to Dr Handley, who was employed by her father's company and had recently moved to the village.

'And this is my baby.' June looked at her mother with distaste whilst limply accepting the man's hand with her unwiped fingers. She jerked her head away when Mrs Trent took a lace-edged handkerchief from her sequin evening bag and attempted to wipe a morsel of cress from her cheek. Dr Handley beamed. 'I've got a niece about your age; she sometimes comes down here for weekends; you must meet her next time; she is going through a horsy phase at present; do you like riding?' 'We sometimes go to the stables at Lyndhurst,' June muttered to her feet.

The band struck up again – a slow foxtrot – while Mrs Trent coquettishly declined the doctor's invitation to dance. 'Do you mind if I sit this one out? I haven't danced so much since I was a young girl. Why don't you ask June? She is a wonderful little dancer.' He inclined his head towards her and smiled, and June momentarily stiffened with fright. She stood woodenly in his arms, mentally whispering to herself 'Slow, slow, quick, quick, slow.' Then he swept her into the centre of the hall, leading her with grace and ease. The taffeta and net swirled from her waist. She pictured herself as Jack Beeston would be seeing her – she knew he must be watching. 'Out of my dreams and into my heart' played the band. Her cheeks felt cool as she cut intricate patterns, deftly avoiding other couples who merely loped to and fro. She even felt happy, and quite beautiful. At last the music stopped, hands clapped and June caught sight of her reflection in the mirror on the wall opposite. Her face looked flat and pale as bread and butter; her dress hung limply as an old net curtain.

She sat down on the nearest chair, mechanically thanking Dr Handley who praised her dancing and repeated the information about his young niece before he left her. She watched the village boys round the bar, snuggling up to the giggling girls in their flowery art-silk dresses, their waists pinched in by tight sashes or wide black belts. Jack Beeston was nowhere to be seen.

The GIs came in. Four over-tall, hulking shapes, tight trousered, khaki bottomed and chewing wads of gum. Mrs Trent cut across the empty floor to where they stood. 'How nice to see you boys; we heard that you were stationed nearby.' They smiled, nodded, and kept calling her ma'am, then left. 'You know what they say about the Yanks,' Mr Trent said thickly to the Muswells and Dr Handley. 'They are oversexed, overpaid, and over-rated.'

'And over here,' the doctor murmured.

Mrs Trent decided that her husband's drinking might disgrace them all if they stayed much longer. 'We really ought to go now, it's getting awfully late.' After a few gushing farewells, she briskly led the way out of the hall into the village square, while Mr Trent ambled in her wake. Although relieved that the dance was over, he would have liked to have gone on drinking with Dr Handley, who seemed quite a decent chap. The corners of his mouth ached with the fixed smile he had felt forced to wear all evening.

Diana had whisked Eric away earlier in order to have some kissing time on the sitting-room couch before her parents' return. All her boy friends were made to adhere to a strict code of honour during these sessions. Kissing was all right as long as they didn't go too far. Only on rare occasions did she allow them to fondle her breasts.

June lagged some distance behind her parents, relieved when they became shrouded in blackness and she could no longer hear her mother's voice. There were new voices coming from behind now, mixed with yowls, smothered laughter, scraping of feet, wolf whistles. Some of the village boys, sounding drunk.

She felt a hand touch her shoulder. 'May I walk you 'ome, miss?' Jack Beeston's face close to her own proved more of a shock than a thrill. 'You don't wanna be walking 'ome by yourself in the black-out.'

His drunken Hampshire dialect appalled her. She knew the request was the result of a dare. 'I'm all right, thanks.' She started walking quickly, then added daftly, 'I live just at the end here.'

'Christ, as if I didn't know where the Trent castle is by now.' He giggled. ''Ang on a mo while I light a fag.'

She looked behind him, wondering if his cronies were still in the vicinity while he laboriously struck a match to his cigarette. There was no sound.

'You look all right in that pink dress. Getting quite big now, aren't you? How old are you?'

'Fourteen in case you want to know.' She wished she had said fifteen.

''Ave you got a sweetheart?' he leered.

'No, but my sister has.'

'That one! He looks a proper twerp if you ask me. Don't walk so fast, you 'aven't got a train to catch.'

She slowed her pace, desperately thinking of something neutral to say.

'You're Jack Beeston, aren't you?'

'That's right, you once went to school with my sister Shirl.'

She winced. Memories of her two terms at the village school, not to mention her brief and intense friendship with the precocious Shirley Beeston, were still vivid in her mind.

They had reached the high, vicarage-like wall in front of June's home when Jack Beeston propelled her against it, prized her lips open with his tongue and groped under her coat to her breasts. She pulled away, turning her head and gasping. 'Didn't you like that then?' he muttered. She was unable to reply. He grabbed her jaw and, forcing it round towards him, repeated his action, pressing her body against his so that she could hardly breathe. Then he moved back slightly, fumbling with his trousers before pulling her hand down. 'Here, feel this,' he rasped. She stood dumbly with her eyes closed, holding his penis. She was having a nightmare from which she would soon wake.

He began rubbing himself against her. She struggled, heard herself saying 'I've got to go in now' in a strangled, high-pitched voice. He lurched backwards, laughing helplessly and buttoning his flies. Somehow she unlatched the garden gate, ran up the driveway and bounded up the stairs two at a time, not seeing her parents standing in the hallway. 'Don't run like that,' her mother called out, 'it will bring on your asthma.' In her room she lay on her bed and stared at the blackness. Her body froze.

On the floor below, her sister sat up in bed winding the ends of her hair into Dinky curlers. She thought of Eric and smiled. She felt she had reached the stage where she could handle her boy friends and not get into the ghastly sex situation that had happened three years ago this Christmas. She was thirteen at the time, and staying at her aunt's house in London. Adam, a friend of their older cousin Douglas, was twenty-two. One cold morning when her aunt had wanted to clear out the girls' room and she was still only half awake, she had wandered into Douglas's room to find Adam still in bed, reading a copy of *Men Only*. 'What do you want?' he had grunted. 'Auntie said I should go into Douglas's bed because she's making mine. She thought you had both gone out.' 'I haven't gone out! Why not come in with me? It must be cold out there.' The rest of the Christmas holiday she had remained unusually quiet, not even bothering to quarrel with June. When their aunt eventually tucked them both under the rug in their parents' car, she complained, 'Diana didn't even like the pantomime this year.'

Downstairs Mr Trent lumbered around for a while, locking all the doors and window catches. Then he took the opportunity of having a nightcap. His wife had gone to bed. When he came upstairs she was lying on her side, breathing evenly. He dropped a shoe, then climbed into bed and, after a few moments, gently patted her backside. Silently she turned round, lifted her nightdress up to her waist and closed her eyes.

K.

He taught me how to swear. Told me dirty jokes and wrote me my first love letter.

Dear Julie,
I love you. Do you love me?
Keith Pratt likes Diana a good bit and thinks you're not bad. I must close now as someone is knocking on the door.
With love,
K.

He drew a picture of himself in a white sailor suit, and one of me dressed like a flamenco dancer with long curly hair.

The swearing lesson had taken place in a field opposite his house when we were both five years old. Bloody this, bloody that, even bugger. I was so impressed.

'Look at this bloody tire!' he said, pointing to one rotting in the long grass.

When I had to leave him to go home to tea, I stopped at the village sweetshop.

'Can I have a pennyworth of jelly babies?'

'You can only have a ha'pennyworth. Other people want them as well as you.'

I gave her a snooty, dirty look, as befitted the daughter of the boss.

'You bloody tire!' Then I ran.

Later my mother divorced my father and my older sister Marion and I went to live with her in Southampton. K's older brother, I., was my sister's first boy friend. So we were both saddened.

When we returned home to stay with my father during the school holidays, he told us that we were to have nothing more to do with the McGregor boys. The reason, we later discovered, was that their parents had been drinking-pals of my drinking mother.

One of those happy life chances occurred some years after that when we were between schools.

My father was looking for a suitable boarding school, safe from air-raids; one where we would receive a good education. Being very pedantic, the process took him some time. So we spent a couple of halcyon terms at Mrs S.'s village school, some two miles away.

K. and his brother were both there.

During lessons we were often interrupted by air-raids. There were two shelters in the front garden. Unfortunately K. was in the other one.

One day the German planes were already overhead and the anti-aircraft guns blasting away before the air-raid sirens sounded their warning wail.

We all ran into either shelter. Mrs S., shouting orders

at us not to panic, was totally ignored, and I landed up in K.'s shelter.

One of the big girls started it off. Pushing everyone towards everyone else, making them kiss each other. It was damp in there and so dark that sometimes the girls landed up kissing girls, giggling helplessly.

To this day I don't remember whether or not I got to kiss K.

The scene rather embarrassed me, kissing to order. As for having to kiss girls. . . . I sat in a corner rocking to and fro, singing sentimental songs to myself.

After the raid was over someone 'split' to Mrs S. She lined the girls up in front of the fireplace in the school house, asking who had been doing the kissing.

When it came to my turn Jill, my best friend, stuck up for me. 'She wasn't doing anything, Mrs S. She was just sitting in the corner singing.'

Mrs S. looked puzzled for a moment, before smacking my outstretched hand with a ruler (not very hard). She must have known that I loved K.

The boys were sent 'down to the house' to have their bottoms caned by Mr S., who hated the job anyway.

Another time we had kiss chases in the copse behind the school house. Most of the time the boys chased the girls.

One day I was waylaid by one of the big boys and taken to the boys' special place in a sort of gully. They sat there, about five or six of them, including K.

'Do you love K.?' Gereald, head boy and ringleader, intoned.

'Yes,' I whispered, staring at the muddy ground. Then

they let me go.

On another occasion I tried playing the *femme fatale* without any success at all.

Someone had given me a box of lace-embroidered hankies for Christmas. I took one to school in an envelope in order to drop it in the copse near the boys' place, so *he*'d be bound to find it.

Unfortunately a little red spy, in a little red coat and matching bonnet, was following me.

Each time I took the hankie from its envelope to let it flutter onto the path, up she came.

'You've dropped your hankie, Julie.' I gave up in the end.

When I was thirteen I came down with pneumonia. My stepmother was furious because she was of the opinion that I had neglected my cold. My father joined forces, saying that I had gone outdoors with my hair wet. He used to try and dry my hair after I'd shampooed it, nearly knocking my head off.

Those were the days before antibiotics. I had M & B tablets and had to sweat it out.

One night a bat flew into the window and I screamed until my father came up. I ducked under the bedclothes while he swatted at it with my green chenille dressing-gown.

Every night or morning, I fell out of bed having epileptic fits.

My stepmother tried to tell my father about it, but he couldn't accept the fact, having endured too many tragedies in his life.

It wasn't until he saw me writhing on the floor that he had to believe it.

When I was recuperating Marion burst into my sickroom with I. He must have been fourteen or fifteen at the time. He sat on the right-hand side of my bed, laughing and talking non-stop, while Marion sat on the end.

He told us a funny anecdote. They had been doing *Julius Caesar* at his school in Southampton. When he had to say 'Friends, Romans, countrymen, lend me your ears,' his prompter 'friend' in the wings stage-whispered 'holes'. So he stood in his toga saying 'holes' and roaring with laughter all through the soliloquy.

I never saw him again. But I saw K. once more, when I was sixteen, on the ferry boat coming back from Southampton to Hythe. He was the one to recognize me.

He looked so different, thin, grey-faced, reflecting the sky.

We were both shy but managed to exchange some information about our lives since we had last met. Sitting far apart on the open deck, I told him that I was going to art school in Southampton, and that I wanted to be a dress designer. He was studying to be a cook.

I don't remember saying goodbye.

Koibito (Lover)

Toshio didn't care anymore, everybody noticed it. His sister told him he was behaving irresponsibly. He shrugged it off. On one occasion he was rude to his parents. Having saved 200,000 yen, he was about to take off for Europe. His elder brother had done so two years ago; they had only received one letter. Meanwhile Toshio fantasied. He had plenty of time to do that whilst slaving at the factory day after day, testing what his father referred to as 'those things'. Mother had been proud of him once, never thinking he would get any sort of job after wasting his time at Tokyo University.

'Toshio makes 25,000 yen a week at the electrical factory.'

'What does he do?'

'He tests torches. If it weren't for him, not one of them would leave the assembly line.'

How bored he became, watching the 'torches' proceed to infinity along the grey belt. It wouldn't be so bad if they merely disappeared, or drifted up to Heaven. But knowing that they all fell in a heap at the end of the line to be plucked up by deft female hands and put into orange and white boxes, seemed so anti-climactic.

There was one particular pair of female hands, attached to one pair of slender arms – Akiko. What a wasted talent. Akiko, whose madonna hands were made

for flower arranging and gentler arts. Akiko, whose eyes
had fixed themselves on Toshio's. Her parents had dis-
owned her when she'd had them operated on to western-
ize her gaze. It didn't stop her from looking at him. Like
kittens and puppies they frolicked together in the hotel
room.

One day, a week before Toshio was due to fly away,
he broke the daily routine. He grabbed a 'torch' from its
conveying-to-eternity belt, took it into the men's lavatory,
wanked and measured himself, and was gratified *his* was
just as long. He giggled before sneaking it back to the
noisy factory floor, and watched it go all the way. And
there was Akiko, bending down to pick it up from the
heap at the end.

That night Akiko's husband stood in the doorway,
waiting. He shivered, but his body was not as cold as
the knife blade pressed to his ribs. A thank-you present
for Toshio's cuckolding activities. Carefully planned, it
was relatively easy to plunge it into his friend's guts.
Blood gushed and flowed along the pavement into the
gutter. Toshio's spirit hovered, flew upwards, took a
sharp right turn, and dive-bombed the factory, landing
unexploded in the orange and white box.

What puzzled Sidney each morning after opening up
the shop, was that the lid of the box was always open.
Unlike so many of his Soho colleagues, he was a methodi-
cal man; it wasn't as if he had put the batteries in, as
with the demonstration model. A customer came in one
lunchtime, peered through the books and magazines,

roamed around a bit touching and fondling the goodies,
made his selection.

'I'll have one of these. It's for the wife, you know.'

'How amazing,' Sidney said.

Jennifer was horrified, disgusted, and don't let's mention
her fury.

'Take that horrid thing away.'

She turned on her right side in the twin bed. Next
afternoon she ransacked the bedroom, finding it at last
among his socks. Buzz, it fell to the floor and waited. She
picked it up, screwed the end sharp right turn, gingerly
trying, gingerly testing, spread-eagled on her back, sigh-
ing impatiently – it wouldn't go in – rummaged on her
dressing table, pot of skin food. It was quite nice once
you got used to it, very nice, or as Edwin would say:
'Bloody marvellous.'

Edwin enquired: 'How's Charlie?'

'Charlie who?'

'You know, the boy friend I bought you.'

'Oh him, that awful thing, I think you're disgusting.'

On pain of death she would never confess to going
to bed with Charlie. Theirs was a clandestine affair,
restricted solely to the afternoons, and she certainly didn't
call him Charlie. He was a nameless rapist, black haired,
wild eyed, whispering obscenities, hairy chest, muscular
stocky, definitely working class. There were also others
– a coloured man (no, a black man). They came in all
shapes and sizes, cajoling, hurling insults. Sometimes a
whole legion came round all at once and stood round the

bed, watching, taking orderly turns. She embraced every one.

Edwin suspected she had Charlie, but had long ceased to tease her about it. Disgruntled, growing a beer-belly, he complained to a friend in a pub : 'She won't let me have it anymore.'

Edwin and Jennifer Lucas request the pleasure of your company on Friday, March 29, at 6.30 p.m. Cocktails, RSVP. Instead of cocktails, British Cream Sherry was to be dispensed to their various sets of friends and in-laws.

Jennifer's canapés looked dainty and colourful but were curiously tasteless, their sogginess the result of having been prepared before her visit to the hairdresser. Bella Simms told her they were 'such lovely eats'. Some other female friend admired her cocktail dress.

'I have a treasure of a modista, she runs these things up for me from time to time.'

'It costs me a bloody fortune,' Edwin said, pouring himself another sherry.

'Oh, but it's worth it, you like your wife to look beautiful, don't you, darling?' contributed his mother-in-law.

Even his mother was forced to admit that the dress looked nice, in spite the fact that it was expensive.

'Nobody tells me I look nice.' He tried to sound jolly.

'That goes without saying, we all think you are beautiful.' Natasha, Jennifer's best friend, sneered assurance.

Edwin was getting bored. The skin between his fingers felt sticky and his head ached. How he hated these do's.

Especially the aftermath. Having to clear up the mess with his hangover, denying he even had one, assessing the damage to his property.

'Why don't those bastards use ash-trays for once instead of burning up my carpets?' 'Which one of your pals put his drink on this leather table top?' Whipping the tacky glass away. 'Good grief, it's not as if I didn't put out plenty of drip-mats.'

'Oh, Mrs Thingy will clear up the mess tomorrow.'

'Mrs Thingy, as well we both know, does fuck all. Why on earth you can't organize your chars to do some housework occasionally, baffles me. I pay them enough.'

He sneaks a large whisky for himself. Jennifer spots it and gives him a filthy look. He downs some of it and stares back at her.

Lawrence wafted over and gazed at her cleavage, then into her eyes.

'You look devastating, Jennie dear. It takes more than a modista to accomplish such a renaissance.'

Jennie blushed, her mother smiled, swiftly tucking her daughter's brassiere strap out of sight.

JENNIFER : 'That's truer than you think.'

LAWRENCE : 'I know what it is. You've got a lover.' (Laughter.)

EDWIN'S MOTHER : 'What a thing to say.'

The party has divided into two camps; Jennifer has more soldiery on her side and more ammunition. Edwin pours himself another sherry, spills some on the carpet, and proceeds to rub it in with his handkerchief. Then, to everyone's amazement, he bounds up the stairs. Jennifer looks embarrassed.

JENNIFER (aside): 'The beast has gone up to be sick.'

NATASHA (grabbing her husband's arm): 'It's been such fun, but we must fly. We are going on somewhere else.'

She kisses Jennifer on the cheek. Jennifer seems distraught, she does the rounds with the sherry decanter. The trenchermen, now leaderless, form small, whispering groups. Edwin comes slowly down the stairs, ceremoniously bearing Charlie on a silver salver.

EDWIN: 'Here's her lover in case anyone is interested.'

He tips him onto the floor, before trampling and smashing him into the Persian rug.

The rout. The field is practically deserted except for Edwin who stands swaying slightly, looking startled. Jennifer crouches weeping over Charlie's earthly remains.

Jennifer accused Edwin of murder. He felt ashamed and guilt-ridden. Having made one or two attempts to justify his behaviour, he tried different tactics. He bought her a large bouquet of mixed flowers.

'Anyone would think it was my funeral,' she sniffed.

The perfume she accepted with some grace. It was the champagne dinner at the 'Gay Hussar' that finally won the day. Edwin sighed with relief when at last he left her bed at two a.m., hoping that the ghost of Charlie was laid for ever. Seldom had a husband's aspirations been so fully realized.

'You've lost weight, old chap. Been on a fat farm?'

'I wish I had, I could do with a rest.' His hand shook as he passed his friend a drink from the bar. Hollow-eyed, pale as a mushroom: 'It's Jennifer. She can't get enough of it, you know.'

London A-Z:
Pages from a Journal

SATURDAY. The row started about money, Jake looking through my cheque book. It soon degenerated into a slanging match. 'The way you throw my money about, keeping all the bums in town I suppose, not to mention the amount you spend up at that pub.' 'All right then, what about the fifty pounds you shelled out for Melanie what's-her-name's abortion?' 'It was only twenty-five quid as it happens; besides, I couldn't afford to take the risk at the time. Since we're muck-raking, what about you? You've got involved with some pretty sordid types, haven't you?'

We were really getting into the thick of it when Ariel came in, carrying a pile of university textbooks, giving us each a look that could mean anything. She put a rock music record on the turntable, squatting on her haunches, spreading out her notes.

I go out to the kitchen and survey the mess, noisily stack up the dishwasher and feel like crying with rage.

Burst into the living-room to shriek about having to do all the washing up all the time. Empty. Remember worn dialogue between myself and Jake. 'What are you moaning about? You've got a dishwasher now, haven't you?' 'Yes, but that doesn't do pots and pans, nor does it tidy up the kitchen.' 'The reason this kitchen gets into such a bloody awful mess is entirely your own fault;

you never put anything away as you go along when you're cooking.' Don't agree with his criticism, some of my creativity is born of chaos. Nevertheless, one side of me hates the untidy squalor. Think of mother-in-law's pristine flat, gleaming skirting boards, lavatory sweetener, no cooking smells, bright expectant smile. Don't expect Ariel to help, she's swotting for exams. Young Josie is out with her first boy friend, Mike. The only time the place looks tidy nowadays is when she asks him back for dinner; then furious carpet-sweeping, tidying-up, emulating his parents' home.

I climb onto the kitchen stool to put some things away on the shelf above the working surface. Smash my forehead on the ever-open cupboard door. Reeling with pain and rage, clutching my brow and swearing, blood oozing from my fingers, I swab with dishcloth, run upstairs to the bathroom. Shiny white lump and cut, pain, eyes watering. At last find plaster dressing loose in medicine cupboard, try sticking it on, no good, wet fingers, loathsome appearance. Rub make-up on lower part of my face whilst combing my hair, look out of window. Downstairs there are three of them now. Josie, my youngest daughter returned home, sits cross-legged, scowling, picking skin off her big toe. Ariel is reading a newspaper, pages are scattered everywhere. Notice with small satisfaction that Jake's eyes don't move from one spot on the page of his book.

I cycle slowly down the Embankment, stop and look at houseboats. Some look lived-in. Flower pots, bright curtains, their smug cosiness like cottages of gingerbread and sweets. They must be inhabited by witches. But

there is a derelict one, black and grey, waddling on its
moorings like a loose tooth in a crone's mouth. It's
called *Orpheus*. I thought all boats had female names.
Grey too the one next to it, an old mine-sweeper with
young people on deck. Girls in blue denims lounging
in deck-chairs, two boys up the mast stringing out bunting, one of the girls waves at me. I cup my hands over my
mouth : 'What do the flags say?' She looks up, questions
the boys, then shouts back, but the answer is lost in the
breeze.

Pedal at stroller's pace down Cheyne Walk, stop at
large police notice outside tall, elegant house. Twisted
arms of wisteria branch off to left and right, holding
house in vice as if propping it up. The notice asks anyone who observed a person or persons leaving these premises between the hours of midnight and two a.m. on
the night of 14 February, to get in touch with the police.
Apparently a woman aged eighty-six was found blud-
geoned to death in the basement flat. Remember reading
something about it in the evening paper.

I turn left into the King's Road. Think of final
moments of threadbare life. Rheumy stare, slack-lipped
horror, repeated blows on wispy skull. Rummaging
through chest of drawers, stale sweaty smell of old
woman's clothes. A stiff ancient handbag crammed full
of snapshots : where does the old bitch keep her money?
Four stinking quid and a few pennies rolled up in a
pair of stockings, look at her lying there, can't be dead.
Didn't hit hard, someone will come and fix her up,
maybe one of the people in the photos. She's gone a
funny colour. Get out quick.

I chain my bike outside the antique market, go inside
and browse through some coloured prints. I would like
to buy one of them. A mountain scene, misty grey-green,
but it's five pounds. Upstairs among second-hand clothes
I fondle chiffon blouse, red and yellow flowers, cigarette
burn on front, smile of recognition. Find treasure of old
umbrellas, parasols, walking-sticks, ivory and silver-
handled. 'How much?' 'Fifteen pounds.' Roof cafeteria
and a glass of lemonade, tame London sparrows on the
scrounge, spread-out remnants of someone's cheese sandwich on the parapet. Fat fluffy one gets most of it. Go
back home. They are still there on the sundeck looking
relaxed, unaware that I have returned. I feel a surge of
anger as I physically try to exorcize black mood by
gardening.

Down in the back yard I have to climb onto a dustbin
in order to reach the flat garage roof. Proceed to tear
down the dead part of the clematis; it's a grimy task. I
lie on the roof, leaning over, brandishing a carving knife.
I would have thought that one of them would ask me
what I was doing, but no. I sweep up the mess and throw
it in the dustbin.

Go to the kitchen and wash my hands. now I'm
ravenous. Grab food at random from the fridge and
gobble most of it down – rollmops, mortadella cheese,
what a mixture. Hiccups. Please God don't let me get
hiccups. Only pray when I'm in a jam or want something, force of habit. The saint who looks after un-
believers mercifully takes heed. The remnants of the
horrid meal are forced down the disposal unit.

Jake has gone into the bathroom to shower, his tran-

sistor going full blast. Top of the Pops and shallow disc
jockey laughing nervously at his own bad jokes. We are
getting to be like the man and woman in the weather-
house, one is in while the other one's out. I go into
the bedroom, quick change, clean teeth, give my armpits
a wipe, stroll downstairs trying to appear nonchalant, not
to give a damn. There they are, glued to the television,
news is on, Ulster bombs. Decide to go up to the pub but
find it far too crowded and noisy for my present humour.
Struggle to the bar and order half a lager. I see Tom,
who reminds me of Olaf from the e. e. Cummings poem,
tall, deep voice, hairy, bearded, direct blue gaze. He tells
me he's feeling randy. 'The next female possibility who
comes in here I'll be in like Flynn.' His arm is around
some girl whose arse is half off the bar stool. 'What makes
you think the next girl will go berserk about you anyway?' I regret that almost immediately. Up and down
look from Tom. 'Give her the stool, she is getting on in
years.'

Go back home after three-quarters of an hour. Jake
says : 'I didn't expect you so soon.' Go to bed. After a
while he comes in, puts on light, makes some notes, lights
off, lumbers around the room a bit, then falls into bed.
Sighs, rattle of sleeping-pills bottle, finally I hear him
breathing evenly. Squeeze my eyes shut, my feet are
cold, curl up, get out of bed, find sweater on floor,
wrap up my feet, shut my eyes, remember what Barbara
Cartland once said, think beautiful thoughts, what beautiful thoughts? Arms around ghost lover no good. Jake's
breathing becomes gentle snores. Listen for a while,
then am in old familiar territory, no longer so frighten-

ing, getting lost on journeys, trains, London buses. A bit
different now, mountains, rocks, greenery, reminiscent of
a landscape.

SUNDAY. Get up late after staring mindlessly at the
papers, shower, stare out of window. Oh no. Close my
eyes in despair, half the clematis is dying, must have
broken one of the main stems. Five years of watching
it grow, trailing it over an arbour. I rig up an old kettle
full of water and immerse the broken stem, hoping it will
grow new roots. I start cooking the Sunday lunch.

Jake leaves the house about midday. He is off to a pub
in South Kensington where we often go together to meet
old friends, couples mostly. I eat lunch on the sundeck
with Ariel and Josie. Ariel and I chatter like magpies,
appreciate each other's company, more since she has
gone to university. How much happier she seems. She
shows me some colour slides of herself and her boy friend.
With other friends, on the campus, in their flat, childlike
poses, she on Ossie's shoulder, laughing, one of him
balancing on his head, poker faced. Many shots of the
distinguished black American poet. Remember my stu-
dent days, parents, almost total lack of freedom, bad
health, lack of boy friends, romantic childhood fantasies,
habit-forming. I'm carried into later years and marriage,
nourished by a sense of alienation.

Jake returns home rather drunk. ME : 'Did you have a
nice lunch out dear?' JAKE, coldly: 'Yes thank you.'
ARIEL, softly : 'It's partly your fault, why do you have to
antagonize him?' I rummage for the Sunday papers, find

what I'm looking for. JAKE : 'I think I had better go and see my father, I phoned him earlier, apparently his back's got worse, you don't have to go unless you want to.' ME : 'I think the children ought to go, they haven't been for a while.' But Josie is going out with Mike. However, Ariel agrees to go as she hasn't seen her grandparents for some time. Jake says he isn't going until early evening, anyway. Meanwhile he continues drinking and puffing at a small cigar, which only serves to make him moodier. He is working himself up towards a confrontation. I pour myself a glass of white wine and offer to make him some coffee. He nods and grunts, brushing ash off his trousers. In the kitchen I look through the entertainment guide : Mahler at the Festival Hall. Take Jake his coffee and put one of my records on the hi-fi. JAKE : 'Why don't you have a rest?' ME : 'I'm not a child and don't treat me like one.' Mike phones for Josie. Jake answers. He calls out : 'Take it on the upstairs phone.' He is beginning to slur. Now for it. 'Why don't you stop drinking?' Silence, more puffing and sipping, if only he would drink the coffee instead. Josie appears, breathless, wearing pretty clothes and too much make-up. 'I've been invited to Mike's place for supper, I'll be back at nine-thirty.' Jake stares at me, I can't stare back, glad there's a vase of flowers on the table between us. I turn up the record-player. 'Isn't it lovely? It's my new record.' Back to trouser brushing and embarrassed downward gaze. JAKE : 'I think we ought to have a talk about our relationship.' ME : 'What's the point?' He puffs some more : 'Well you said yourself that the past conditions us, you know.' ME : 'Yes I know, but it's no good croaking on about the past when we're trying to live in the present, it's all so futile.' I'm beginning to shout. JAKE : 'The trouble with you is that as soon as I want to have a quiet discussion about our relationship, you always lose your temper.' ME : 'But we can't keep rehearsing the same old issues each time, we don't seem to make much progress anyway. If you had been more honest with me in the past we wouldn't have got into such a mess in the first place.' JAKE : 'Honest? It's not exactly easy being honest with you, not even now.' ME : 'Honesty tends to hurt, doesn't it? Anyway, women have to be devious, too, it's the only way they can survive half the time.' There's a pause. Jake stubs out the remaining quarter inch length of cigar, flicks the invisible dust from his sleeve. 'Well, what is it that you are hiding from me?' I give an exasperated sigh and exit up the stairs, trying not to answer him.

I go to the lavatory, already regretting sounding so enraged. I'm not going to apologize to him now, especially as he is drunk. My nerves are jangling. I go into the bedroom and stare at my reflection, parchment lines, deep-set, alarmed gaze. I'm beginning to see the resemblance to my older sister. Hear the front door slam, look out of the window and watch them getting into the car. I feel I should have gone too, but am unable to tolerate his company for the time being. Anyway, I decided earlier to go to the chamber-music recital at the Queen Elizabeth Hall. Shower, change into a long mauve skirt and peasant blouse. Make up face, carefully avoiding the wound on my forehead, but succeed in reopening it with my comb. Bloody hell! Dab styptic pencil on it to stop it bleeding. At Earl's Court Underground wait ten minutes, no train. A young couple had already been waiting for fifteen minutes to get refunded. Friendly Japanese acquaintance waves at me as I climb into a taxi.

I begin to relax, trees in blossom in the garden squares. London seems so lovely. Plenty of time to get there, it should be easy to get a ticket on a Sunday. Anyway, there's always the Purcell Room, or even Mahler at the Festival Hall. We're cruising down St James's, what a sight on a warm spring evening. Wish I had someone to share it with. Alan, my lover, who no longer loves me. But I can't let him go, he's nice to me, takes me out from time to time. How he's changed, I suppose I have, too. No longer the intimate little Soho restaurants and concerts, now it's meals at the Royal Garden Hotel, or somewhere equally large and impersonal. No chance to get emotional in those places. He seems so brittle and matter-of-fact nowadays. Almost impossible to believe what our relationship was like once. People strolling in the park. I see with absolute astonishment a white-haired man and woman in what must be their so-called middle years, cuddling on the grass. Turn round and stare through the tinted rear window, so amazed and impressed that tears never enter my mind.

A great queue has formed outside the Festival Hall for Mahler returned tickets. No hope there. Not much time, either. Smallish queue at the Queen Elizabeth Hall, kept in order by friendly Irish official. I start talking to continental man behind : 'This is almost as bad as Covent Garden.' 'Nothing is as bad as Covent Garden.'

Singles are sorted out and I finally get in. Find it difficult to concentrate on the music at first, string quartets,
Haydn and Mozart. After the first piece the audience
indulge in an orgy of coughing and nose blowing. Remember the row, guilt, blame, antagonism. I must listen.

Interval. Bar. Glass of wine. Look down at the Thames,
ducks flying up river, expanse of deep blue sky, chunky
huddled clouds. I am able to concentrate more during
the second half of the programme. Guest artists enthrall-
ing. I linger in the foyer gathering leaflets for concerts
I'm never likely to attend. Rather like picking bluebells
in a wood, knowing they will be dead before I get them
home.

Half-way back in the underground I get out on
impulse to call on Alan, ostensibly to tell him about the
concert. Must be three months now, after all we're still
supposed to be good friends, why not? I stare up at his
window for some time, he's there all right. Ring the bell.
I must try to sound casual, as if I've just seen him recently and nothing has changed. 'Hi there, just been to a
marvellous concert at the Queen Elizabeth Hall.' 'Hullo
Julia. Do you know what time it is?' He bars the doorway, clutching a copy of the *London A-Z*. 'It's all right
for you, you stay in bed half the morning but I've got to
get up early.' My frown causes a flickering pain on my
forehead. I stand back. 'OK, forget I came.' I walk
quickly up the road and hail a taxi, past the glittering
shops, closing my eyes.

Back home lights everywhere, people hanging out of
windows opposite, revolving blue flicker from police car
in front of house. I feel everything dropping from me.

Heart thudding in my ears. Jake. Ariel. The car. Somehow I get up the steps and fumble with the keys. Drop them at least twice. Get in. The house is in darkness. I lean against the door, feeling sick with fright. The light goes on. Ariel is standing at the top of the stairs with bath-towels wrapped around her head and body. 'Oh God, are you drunk again?' Later, after I've got over the shock, I explain that I thought there had been a car accident because of the police car. 'Oh that, no, it's the woman next door, the one that's married to the old Pole. Apparently he beat her up and when she screamed they called the cops. I gather she was having it off with somebody.' 'Where's Daddy?' 'Well, Cyril phoned and he's gone off to the Elm.'

I get undressed and into bed without removing my make-up or cleaning my teeth, feeling completely drained. My feet are freezing and I'm wearing my dressing-gown and winter nightie. Finally I have to get up and fetch a thick sweater to wrap my feet in. Curl up and try to go to sleep. But my mind is racing along, full of dialogue. Try daydreaming, usual romantic nonsense but better than sleeping pills. Getting warmer and drowsy. Phone rings, grope for the receiver. 'Hullo, it's me.' There's a terrible background racket so he's shouting. 'I'm with Cyril and Sue. We're at a party at Yoshi's, their Japanese pal. Do you want to come? They're all asking for you.' His voice sounds thick. 'No, I'm in bed.' 'Wait a minute, Sue wants to speak to you.' Pause. Sue gets on the phone, she sounds shrill. 'Why don't you come?' 'I can't, Sue, I'm dreadfully tired, I'll phone you tomorrow. Goodnight.' Click.

I Think I'm Going Crazy

That's what A. said when he telephoned her. It sounded so garbled that Minnie thought he *must* be going that way. It took her a long time to get the gist of it.

Apart from being her male char and one of her best friends, he also 'did' for another of her best friends, a lady professor in fact. Minnie had recommended him highly. 'The Japs are bloody marvellous. He's the third I've had.'

Professor B. giggled. 'Minnie's got a gigolo.'

Some professor!

A. had the keys to Professor B.'s flat, as she was out much of the time. She found some of her students worthwhile, others distinctly lacking in brain-power. All the while she smoked her academic head off, giving up only when her voice began to croak and finally fade away to a husky whisper in the middle of a lecture.

Besides cleaning for Professor B. and Minnie, A. had other, more pleasurable duties. He had two beautiful Japanese girl friends. One of them couldn't bear to be left behind in Tokyo without him, so she hopped on a plane. Her parents were horrified as they had other plans for their twenty-year-old only child; Toshi, a nice respectable young man of twenty-seven, would have made a perfect son-in-law.

P., the other Japanese beauty, was twenty-four and petite. She had been in swinging London for some time, working in bars, doing odd jobs and, lately, trying her hand at being a mother's help. She flatly refused to speak Japanese which proved terribly confusing for A. Mercifully she occasionally lapsed into Japanese when they were in bed together, whispering words of love.

A. and some of his Japanese friends were fortunate in renting rooms from M.L. at very reasonable rates. He was a delightful elderly gentleman, patient and sympathetic, who collected oriental antiques. Every room in the small flat was full of his treasures. A. and his friends took care of them and of the old gentleman as well, as he suffered from arthritis and did not find it easy to move about.

To get back to the beginning, and to A.'s reason for thinking that he was going crazy.

One day, as he was wandering round Professor B.'s flat wishing he could get a good night's sleep sometime soon, the Australian tenant from the basement flat rang the doorbell.

He came straight to the point. 'Can I borrow your vacuum cleaner, old sport?'

Because of the language barrier, he had to repeat his request several times. Finally A. understood. 'You are a friend of the Professor?'

The Aussie looked flummoxed. Finally he grabbed A.'s

hand and shook it vigorously. He departed with the vacuum cleaner.

That was on a Monday. He returned it the same day, but was back again the following Monday looking somewhat hung over.

'We had a bit of a party last night and the place looks like the bottom of a parrot's cage. Could I borrow the vacuum again, matey?'

A. handed it over and shut the door. 'I must go and wash the kitchen floor,' he murmured sleepily.

'Where's my vacuum cleaner?' asked the lady professor.

'The gentleman downstairs, he come up and ask me to let him have it for a short time.'

Then all hell broke loose. Lady professors, being clever and professional people, don't suffer fools gladly. Professor B. told A. that he had done a daft thing.

A. told Minnie over the telephone. 'I will have to go.'

'Go where?' croaked Minnie. It was early in the morning, nine-thirty or thereabouts.

'Go leave Professor B.'

'Why?'

'Because it was because of you I get the job.'

Minnie wanted to ask 'What the hell are you talking about?', but she refrained. She thought it might be bad form to swear when her Japanese friend appeared so distraught. Finally her sleep-fuddled brain grasped that the vacuum had gone missing, but before she could offer any helpful suggestions he had hung up.

She sat huddled in her green armchair next to the telephone, trying to think of a plan to restore relations between A. and Professor B. Then she went upstairs and sat on the porcelain rim of the lavatory bowl where she had had some of her best ideas in the past. As her husband's uncle had once declared: 'Man's great ideas are often formulated on the lavabo seat.'

She would buy A. a new bloody vacuum. She grinned to herself anticipating the row that would take place if her husband got wind of her plans.

'Christ Almighty! You spend money like bloody water. We're supposed to be economizing, anyway.'

'But it's my money, not the housekeeping.'

'I can just imagine how happy your father would be if he knew you intended to blow thirty quid on a Hoover for one of the Yellow Peril.'

She would buy a Hoover Junior and tell A. that she had purchased it for a fiver (lie) from one of her pub friends in the King's Head, and that it had fallen off the back of a lorry (lies again). Minnie prided herself on being an excellent liar, especially when her back was against the wall.

She went to Barkers early the next morning, eleven-thirty to be exact, which was unusual for her at the best of times. Hoping she wasn't over-drawing on her bank account, she bought the Hoover Junior and took it home in a taxi.

After hearing A.'s tale of woe, M.L. was similarly inspired with an idea. He took a taxi to Harrods and returned the same way, even more heavily laden than Minnie as he had purchased the larger model.

A.'s pretty petite girl friend, P., had recently started a lousy job with lousy employers, looking after two lousy brattish brats aged ten and twelve. When they weren't fighting with each other, the boys invariably took it out on her, like two pummelling bullies. The six-month-old baby was all right, except that she naturally involved P. in a great deal of work. At the same time the bossy bosses piled more and more work onto P., like doing all the washing up and cleaning out the dustbins twice a week. One day when they handed her the lavatory brush, she decided to pack it in and do a moonlight flit. Remembering how grief-stricken A. had seemed the last time she saw him, she took her slave-driving employers' cylindrical model with her when she left.

As she crept from the house, heavily burdened by the suitcase and the awkwardly-shaped vacuum, she felt sorry for the baby of whom she had grown rather fond.

Minnie succeeded in dragging her Hoover Junior round to Professor B.'s doorstep around midday. Professor B.'s younger daughter tore herself away from her sweet lover's arms to open the door. 'It's all right, we got the Hoover back,' she muttered sleepily, before shutting the door in Minnie's face.

Minnie's Hoover Junior went back to Barkers.

M.L.'s model was returned to Harrods.

The cylindrical machine was dumped in the street.

Mickey Mouse

'Woman, will you get away from dat window and come back to bed!' Her latest lover, from Trinidad, was already beginning to sound possessive.

'M-m-m', she murmured, closing the window as a slight concession, but continuing to stare out.

She was intrigued by the comings and goings of the new male tenants in the basement flat. Originally there were supposed to be three of them, but they seemed to be multiplying overnight.

She finally climbed back into bed and absently began stroking Monty's woolly head.

'I let the place to three young Japs and now there seem to be umpteen of them. Talk about the Yellow Peril,' she grumbled.

But Monty wasn't interested in her problems, as he brusquely set out to prove. She was relieved when he finally left to meet up with some of his West Indian friends in a drinking club in Ladbroke Grove.

She gave Luke, her five-year-old son, his supper.

'I don't like him,' Luke said between mouthfuls.

'What?'

'I don't like him, your nig-nog.'

'Well you don't have to, he's *my* friend.'

He gave her a dirty look and continued munching. Later he made more than his usual fuss about going to bed.

Stella Hobbs was unmarried and talked volubly about the advantages of being so. Neverthless, she secretly wished that she could find someone who was a little more than passing trade.

She lived with Luke's father for three fighting years. On reflection it seemed infinitely longer.

Luke, like his mother, was very strong-willed. Their battles never ceased, and sometimes they threw things at each other.

Although Stella was only thirty-six, she felt that she was beginning to look several years older. For one thing she was too thin and drawn-looking. She occasionally wondered if she should study Yoga or Zen, but was far too disorganized to do anything about it.

Financially, she wasn't too badly off. Luke's father had left them a reasonably-sized house in Shepherd's Bush, and although it was dilapidated, it had a basement flat which she was able to let furnished. But there was invariably trouble with the tenants, whom she chose as haphazardly as she picked her lovers. Some had done moonlight flits, pinching the cutlery or the bedclothes. The last lot had been Australians, who left having paid the rent but owing a considerable sum for overseas telephone calls. Then someone had told her that the Japanese were clean and reliable.

In the beginning, the three of them would all come upstairs together, to pay the rent or to make minor

requests in smiling pidgin English. Now there appeared
to be five or possibly more. She decided to create when
they started moving in their girl friends. That was when
the trouble had started with the Aussie crew. Continual
late night rave ups, and one of the girls sobbing on her
doorstep one wintry night, complaining about the way
her boy friend was treating her. In the end Stella had
shut the door firmly in the girl's face. Christ! It wasn't
as if she hadn't troubles enough on that score herself.

She was surprised when, soon after the new tenants
had moved in, the three-man deputation came up and
invited her to tea. One of them pointed Luke and said :
'Little boy too.'

She was amazed at the way they had transformed the
normally shabby basement flat. It was festooned with
multi-coloured origami birds, paper lanterns and orna-
mental scrolls.

'My God, you've done wonders with this place,' she
marvelled.

They smiled and nodded, ushering her to the most
comfortable chair, while they sat cross-legged on the
floor pouring some of the contents of a Teacher's whisky
bottle into glasses. She was handed a glass with a smile :
'Japanese tea.'

She laughed, feeling considerably cheered. They *were*
human after all, asking her to tea and then dishing out
whisky !

'Could I have some ice and water in it ?'

Three blank looks.

'Iced water,' she repeated slowly.

'Ah.' One of them went to the fridge and produced a

milk bottle full of iced water. His movements were graceful and languid, as were his friends'.

She wondered if they were queers. If so, there wouldn't
be any girl friend trouble. And they certainly didn't
look the types who would import bitchy queens onto the
premises.

A glass of iced water was handed to her. She poured
half of it into her whisky and downed a fairly large
gulp. It *was* tea.

'I thought it was whisky.'

They all laughed and began gabbling to each other in
Japanese. She heard her name crop up a couple of
times and began to feel foolish, fervently wishing it had
been whisky.

One of them offered her a plate of chocolate biscuits.
She was unable to look into his small brown eyes. Instead
she stared hard at his T-shirt, with its picture of Mickey
Mouse. Nibbling the chocolate biscuit she didn't want,
drinking the watered-down tea, she wished to hell they
would speak the Queen's English, or serve iced tea from
glass jugs, like civilized people. It all seemed like a bad
oriental joke.

Luke remained mesmerized throughout the entire
proceedings, eating, drinking and imitating his hosts'
good manners extremely well.

When they got up to leave, the Mickey Mouse charac-
ter insisted on escorting them upstairs, saying goodbye
with a swift little bow and a shy smile.

She flopped down on her bed and closed her eyes.
Luke remained unusually quiet for some time.

'What are their names?' he finally asked.

'Christ knows, look in the rent book.' She felt tired. It had all seemed such a strain.

Monty came round later and found her asleep. He shook her awake.

'Woman, have you been on de piss?'

'Yes,' she murmured drowsily, wishing she hadn't given him the spare key.

When she began explaining to him about the Japanese tea in the whisky bottle, he went almost berserk.

'You're one damned crazy woman, d'you know dat? Why, dat stuff's poison. One of me mates was telling me 'bout dat stuff. Dem Goddam Japs used to practically give it away by de gallon at de end of de last war. Dat fuckin whisky turned men blind.'

She sat up rubbing her eyes as Monty lay down beside her with a sigh of despair.

'See woman, it seems like you're going blind already.' He began to snore.

She looked at him for a few moments before climbing over his body.

'I wonder what kind of whisky you've been boozing on,' she muttered as she went into Luke's room.

Luke was sitting cross-legged on his bed, cutting and folding pieces of paper from a *Beano* annual.

'What are you doing?'

'I'm making one of them birds.'

'*Those* birds. What birds?'

'Ziro made one. Look!' He held up a pink origami crane dangling from a cotton thread. 'He says it makes you happy.'

'Well, I hope it bloody well works. What do you want for supper?'

Together they shouted: 'Hamburger and chips.' Without knowing why, Stella felt rather elated as she went out to the shops to buy some food.

Monty had been away for some time doing a gig with his bongo drums in the north of England. He sent a card from Manchester bearing the message: 'It's hard work, but the bread is good. I hope my chick is behaving herself. M.'

Luke had started primary school and would come home tired and more obstreperous than ever. Stella toyed with the idea of getting any kind of part-time job, as the walls were beginning to close in on her. She washed the paintwork, cleaned out cupboards, and tried to persuade herself that it was all so worthwhile. She even took up pottery classes, but found the other ladies far too genteel for her liking. Besides, she was no damned good at it anyway.

She heard their voices in the street outside and gazed down as they came up the front steps. They had indeed multiplied. Now they were bringing in girl friends and carrying guitars.

She crept downstairs and stood outside their door, listening to the music and sounds of gentle merriment.